FEAR STREET
R·L·STINE

Double Date

D0311624

A Parachute Press Book

AN ARCHWAY PAPERBACK
Published by POCKET BOOKS
New York   London   Toronto   Sydney   Tokyo   Singapore

AN ARCHWAY PAPERBACK *Original*

An Archway Paperback published by
POCKET BOOKS, a division of Simon & Schuster Inc.
1230 Avenue of the Americas, New York, NY 10020

Copyright © 1994 by Parachute Press, Inc.

ISBN: 0-671-78570-2

First Archway Paperback printing April 1994

10 9 8 7 6 5 4 3

FEAR STREET is a registered trademark of Parachute Press, Inc.

AN ARCHWAY PAPERBACK and colophon are registered trademarks of Simon and Schuster Inc.

Cover art by Bill Schmidt

Printed in the U.S.A.

IL 7+

Double Trouble

"I think Bree really likes you," Samantha told him.

"I think I like you better," Bobby replied.

"You'd better be careful," she said, avoiding his eyes.

"What do you mean?"

"You'd better be careful not to hurt her," Samantha warned, raising her eyes to Bobby's. "My sister can be a little . . . strange when she's hurt."

Bobby stared hard at Samantha. A cloud drifted over the moon and her face darkened. "What do you mean?"

"I really don't want to talk about it," she told him. "Just be careful with Bree, Bobby. Be very careful."

Books by R. L. Stine

Available from ARCHWAY Paperbacks

chapter

1

School Spirit

*B*obby Newkirk pressed against the locker door with one hand, squeezing Ronnie Mitchell into her locker.

"Ow!" she squealed in protest. "Let me out, Bobby!"

He grinned at her, the devilish grin he had practiced in a mirror. The grin that made girls melt. "Got you trapped."

"Let me out!" Ronnie tried to break free. But she was a little girl, slender and short. Not strong enough to budge him.

Still grinning, he leaned forward and kissed her.

She returned the kiss. He knew she would.

Then she shoved him away, pushing both fists against the broad front of his maroon and white Shadyside High T-shirt.

He laughed and stepped back, allowing her to burst free.

"You're terrible," she scolded playfully, tossing a red curl off her forehead.

"You love it," Bobby replied.

She straightened the bottom of her green T-shirt. "I had fun last night," she murmured shyly, lowering her eyes. Her freckled cheeks reddened.

"Of course," Bobby said, gazing over her shoulder to study himself in her locker door mirror. "You're not bad yourself, babe."

"Don't call me babe," Ronnie told him. "I really hate it. It's so dumb."

"Okay, babe." He leaned forward to kiss her again, but she ducked to the side.

"People are watching!" Ronnie whispered.

"So?" Bobby shrugged his broad shoulders. "Let them be jealous." He glanced into her mirror again and pushed back his straight blond hair. "I've got to run."

Ronnie slipped her backpack onto one shoulder. "Where are you going?"

"Places." Bobby grinned at her. He pulled a piece of lint off the shoulder of her T-shirt. Then he placed it on her little freckled nose.

Ronnie sighed and blew it away. "I'm going to cheerleader practice," she said, glancing at the clock over their heads. Three-twenty. "Want to meet after?"

Bobby shook his head. "Unh-unh." He turned away from her and gazed down the nearly empty hall. "I've got practice too. Catch you later, okay?"

He loped toward the music room at the end of the hall. Bobby moved with a confident, easy gait. He knew Ronnie's eyes were on him. He was sure she was admiring him.

2

"Call me tonight?" Ronnie called after him. There was a pleading tone in her voice.

"Maybe," Bobby muttered. He kept walking.

He liked Ronnie. She wasn't the prettiest girl he had dated. With her tiny figure, red hair, and freckles, she looked about twelve. But she was okay. Kind of fun.

Why had he asked her out? Because she was the only Tigers cheerleader he hadn't gone out with. He had to have a perfect record. He had to check Ronnie off his list.

I've gone out with all six cheerleaders. Bobby grinned to himself. Who *says* I don't have school spirit?

His private joke made him laugh out loud. "I really crack myself up."

All six girls were nuts about me too, Bobby decided.

Maybe I'll call Ronnie again sometime, he thought. Maybe I'll give the kid a break.

Just outside the music room, he stopped to talk to two guys. Jerry Marvin slapped him a high-five.

"What's up?" Markie Drew asked Bobby.

"Where you guys going? Detention?" Bobby joked.

Jerry made a face. "My dad made me get a job. I'm working at McDonald's. Making French fries."

Bobby snickered. "Starting at the top, huh?"

"We don't all have rich parents," Jerry muttered.

"Too bad," Bobby replied smugly.

Markie shifted his backpack to his other shoulder. "You still going with Cari Taylor?" he asked Bobby.

"No, I dumped her," Bobby replied, a wide grin spreading across his handsome face.

Both Markie and Jerry reacted with surprise. "You did?"

Bobby nodded. "Yeah. She spilled Coke in my car. So I dumped her." He chuckled. "Made her walk home too."

"Wow." Markie shook his head.

"Hey, man, can I have your rejects?" Jerry asked.

"Sure. Be my guest," Bobby offered. He gazed distractedly at the music room. "Hey, later. I'm late for practice."

His two friends headed off. Bobby started into the music room.

But two strong hands grabbed his shoulders and pulled him back.

"Bobby, I'm going to kill you!" a shrill voice cried. "I really am!"

chapter

2

"No Problem"

*B*obby laughed. He didn't bother to turn around. He recognized the voice. "Whoa!" he cried. "Don't touch me unless you love me."

Kimmy Bass let out an exasperated cry and pulled her hands from Bobby's shoulders. "Where were you last night?" she demanded angrily.

Bobby spun around to face her. His blue eyes flashed. He opened them wide and gave her his best innocent, little-boy expression. "Last night?"

Kimmy tossed her dark, crimped hair in an angry gesture. Her round cheeks were bright red. She crossed her arms in front of her pale blue sweatshirt. "Yeah. Last night."

Bobby pretended to think about it.

"We had a date, remember?" Kimmy said, her voice trembling. "You were coming over so we could study together. Then we were going to—"

"You look great," Bobby interrupted. "You heading

to cheerleader practice? Want to get a Coke or something later?"

Kimmy let out another groan. She balled her hands into fists at her sides. "Just answer my question, Bobby. I called your house last night, but you weren't there. Did you forget about me?"

"No way," Bobby replied, placing a hand on her shoulder.

She shoved it away.

"Actually," Bobby continued, "I got a better offer." He grinned at her.

Her mouth dropped open. No sound came out.

"Hey, Kimmy, you wouldn't want me to *lie,* would you?"

Kimmy glared at him. The anger faded from her eyes. Her expression turned hard and cold. "Bobby, you really are a pig," she said through clenched teeth.

Bobby snickered. "Yeah, I know."

"You're a pig," Kimmy repeated. Then she began jogging quickly down the hall, her black hair bobbing.

"Hey, Kimmy—" Bobby called after her. "Should I call you later?"

She shouted a curse and disappeared around a corner.

Chuckling, Bobby stepped into the music room.

"Hey, Bobby."

"Get your guitar, man. You're late."

Bobby nodded to Arnie and Paul, the other two members of his band. He went to the cabinet to get his guitar. The three of them had no room to practice at home. Mr. Cotton, the music teacher, had agreed to let them practice in a music room after school.

They had just changed the name of their group from

6

The Cool Guys to Bad to the Bone. In the four months they'd been playing together, the band changed its name at least once a week. Bobby said they spent more time thinking up names than practicing.

Paul, the keyboard player, noodled impatiently on the keys, waiting for Bobby. Paul was broad shouldered and athletic, with dark skin and large brown eyes. He had a surprisingly light touch on the keyboard. He was the hardest-working member of the band and took practice much more seriously than Bobby or Arnie.

Arnie pounded the drums without much skill. The best thing anyone could say about Arnie's drumming was that he kept a steady beat. Most of the time.

Arnie was in the band mainly because he was Bobby's best friend. Arnie had short red hair, pale blue eyes, a goofy grin, and wore a small rhinestone stud in one ear. The line of pale blond fuzz on his upper lip, which he claimed was a mustache, only made him look sloppy.

Bobby plugged his guitar into the small amp. Then he turned up the volume until it squealed. He sat down on a folding chair in front of Arnie and Paul and started to tune each string.

Bobby loved his guitar. It was a white Fender Strat. "The kind Jimi Hendrix used," he told everyone. Arnie once said that Bobby loved his guitar almost as much as he loved himself.

Bobby had reacted defensively. "Hey, man," he shouted, "why *shouldn't* I love myself? I'm all I've got!"

"Very deep," Paul had muttered. "Bobby is sooo deep."

Bobby finished tuning. He bent down and reached into his guitar case for a pick.

"Let's get started," Paul urged. "I've got to leave early to pick my mom up at work."

"Where are my picks?" Bobby said, frowning. "I always leave them in the case. But—"

"Maybe you were picking your nose with them again," Arnie suggested. He let out his high-pitched hyena giggle. No one else laughed. No one *ever* laughed at Arnie's attempted jokes.

"Arnie, you're about as funny as the dry heaves," Bobby muttered, still searching for a pick.

Paul groaned. "Did you forget we're playing at an actual club Friday night?" he demanded.

"Where were you last night?" Arnie asked Bobby, ignoring Paul's question. "Did you go out with Kimmy?"

Bobby turned back to grin at him. "No. Ronnie."

Arnie's pale blue eyes went wide. "I thought you had a study date with Kimmy."

"I did," Bobby replied. "But Ronnie called, and—what can I tell you?" He shrugged. "I can't be two places at once."

Arnie laughed. "You're bad. You're really bad."

"Kimmy will get over it," Bobby said. He found a pick and ran it through the strings a few times.

"I'm surprised you didn't go out with both of them at once," Paul said dryly.

Bobby started to reply, but a movement at the door made him stop. "Hey!" he called out as two girls hesitantly entered the room.

He recognized the Wade twins at once. Everyone at

Shadyside High knew Bree and Samantha Wade. The twins had moved to Shadyside the year before. They had quickly assumed the reputation as the most beautiful girls in the school.

Identical, they both had creamy smooth skin and straight black hair. Perfect hair that shone like in shampoo commercials. They had round green eyes, high cheekbones, and warm, natural smiles.

Bree was shy. She seldom spoke in class. Samantha was more outgoing and lively. The girls had friends, but no close friends. They went out on dates, but neither of them had steady boyfriends.

Strumming the guitar softly, Bobby stared at them as they entered. Bree lingered by the door. Samantha stepped into the center of the room. They were dressed in faded jeans and striped shirts.

They are *cool!* Bobby thought. Earlier in the year, he had thought about asking one of them out. But he just hadn't gotten around to it.

"Is Mr. Cotton here? We're looking for him," Samantha said, her eyes on Bobby.

"No cotton here," Arnie told them. "But I have some Q-Tips in my locker."

No one laughed.

"We haven't seen him," Paul told them.

"He usually clears out when we start to play." Bobby smiled.

Samantha smiled back. Bree had her hands jammed into her jeans pockets. "Maybe he's in the teachers' lounge," she suggested to her sister.

The twins started to leave. "Hey—stay and listen!" Bobby called to them.

9

"We've got to find him," Samantha replied.

Bobby studied them as they made their way back to the hall. Wow, what great bods! he thought.

"What do you want to play first?" Paul asked. He was tapping all his fingers on the edge of the keyboard.

"I want to play *them!*" Arnie declared, meaning the twins.

"They are *hot!*" Bobby agreed. "Did you see the way one of them was checking me out?"

"That's because your fly is unzipped," Arnie joked.

"I can't tell them apart," Paul offered. "Which one was Bree and which one was Samantha?"

"What difference does it make?" Bobby demanded. "They're both totally hot!" He was silent for a moment. "Talk about dating two girls at once! What would it be like to go out with twins? Wow."

Paul shook his head. "Bobby, even you wouldn't do that."

"Sure he would," Arnie said enthusiastically.

"Sure I would," Bobby murmured thoughtfully. "I'd go out with one on Friday and the other one on Saturday. And make them swear not to tell the other."

"No way," Paul insisted.

"Why shouldn't I give each of them a break?" Bobby demanded, warming to the idea. "I mean, why not spread it around? Those two girls have been deprived for too long."

"At least he isn't conceited," Paul muttered dryly.

Bobby spun around to face his two friends. "You don't think I could do it?"

"I think they'd tell each other," Paul replied. "And then they'd tell you to get lost."

"Want to bet?" Bobby demanded heatedly.

Arnie twirled a drumstick in his fingers. He studied Bobby's serious expression. "You really think you could date both Wade twins in one weekend?"

"No problem, guys," Bobby boasted. "No problem at all."

chapter

3

A Warning

"_I_'m late. I've got to run," Paul said. He slid his keyboard into the cabinet. "My mom is going to be waiting in the street."

"Good practice," Bobby commented, his eyes on the heavy gray clouds outside the music room window. "Maybe you guys won't embarrass me Friday night."

"The two _Tommy_ songs need work," Paul said, hurrying to the door. "We weren't together. And the tempo was way too slow."

"Yeah," Bobby agreed. He played a fast riff from one of the _Tommy_ songs. "I've been listening to the CD. That's the right tempo. Same as The Who."

"Who's on first?" Arnie chimed in.

"What's on second" was Bobby's reply.

"I'm out of here," Paul said.

Bobby unplugged the white Fender Strat from the amp. He grinned at Arnie. "Think the Wade twins are still around?"

"You're really going to do it?" Arnie asked.

"You can have them when I'm done," Bobby told him.

"You're a real friend," Arnie joked. He started a drumroll but dropped a stick. It clattered to the floor and rolled in front of Bobby. As Bobby bent to pick it up, he saw Melanie Harris step into the room.

Bobby tossed the drumstick at her. "Think fast!"

Melanie let out a surprised squeal and ducked out of the way. The drumstick hit the wall and bounced across the floor. "Give me a break," Melanie said. She bent to pick up the drumstick, then scowled at Bobby.

Bobby laughed. He watched Melanie as she crossed the room to Arnie. She was a short girl, a little chunky. She had waist-length straight brown hair that she usually wore in a single braid. She had beautiful brown eyes and a great smile.

Bobby had fallen for that amazing smile. The previous spring he had gone out with Melanie for nearly three months. A record for him.

But Melanie stopped smiling at him when she discovered he was dating other girls behind her back. She broke up with him immediately, tears running down her face. She hadn't smiled at him since.

Now she was going with Arnie.

Just as well, Bobby thought. He really didn't like the emotional ones. Why did she have to cry the night she broke up with me? he wondered. Was she trying to make me feel bad?

Bobby watched her as she handed the drumstick to Arnie. She looks great in those tight jeans, he thought. She wore a silky black vest, open, over a golden yellow shirt.

Not bad, Bobby told himself. If she'd lose a few pounds, I might even ask her out again. I mean, when Arnie's finished with her.

Melanie and Arnie were chatting quietly. Bobby carried his guitar to its case to put it away. "You coming Friday night?" he called to Melanie.

"Arnie is forcing me," Melanie replied.

"It's going to be great," Arnie told her. "We had a great rehearsal today. Didn't we, Bobby?"

"Awesome," Bobby replied, clasping the guitar case.

"What do you think we should wear?" Arnie asked. "We never talked about that."

"How about bags over your heads?" Melanie suggested. She snickered. "You know. Just in case your music makes the crowd ugly."

"A bag would mess up my hair," Bobby muttered. He carried the case to the cabinet and shoved it inside.

"I was just kidding!" Melanie exclaimed. She groaned. "You are the vainest person I ever met!"

"Takes one to know one," Bobby shot back. He unplugged the amp and started to roll up the cord.

Melanie and Arnie talked quietly again. Bobby carried the amp to the cabinet and lowered it to the cabinet floor.

He heard girls' voices out in the hall. The Wade twins?

"Got to run," he called to Melanie and Arnie. He started to the door.

"Hey, Bobby—" Melanie called to him. "Don't do it."

14

"Huh?" He turned back. Her dark eyes were trained on him, narrowed in disapproval.

"Stay away from Bree and Samantha," Melanie warned.

Bobby couldn't keep a grin from spreading across his face. "Arnie told you?"

Melanie nodded. "Bobby, I'm warning you," she said. "I know those girls. They're not what you think."

Bobby laughed scornfully. "I can get along without your advice, Mel."

"I'm serious," Melanie insisted. "Stay away from them."

Bobby shook his head hard, as if shaking away her warning. "I'll leave you two *lovebirds* alone," he said sarcastically.

He hurried out of the room. The long corridor was empty. His sneakers squeaked against the hard floor as he started to his locker.

Melanie's warning repeated in his ears. What is her *problem* anyway? he thought. He decided she was still messed up because of breaking up with him.

Melanie hasn't gotten over me yet, he told himself. Well—who can blame her?

As he turned a corner, he nearly banged into an open locker door. He stopped short—and a startled girl appeared from around the other side of the door.

"Hi," he said, recovering quickly, turning on his smile. "Are you Bree or Samantha?"

chapter

4

One Down

She gaped at him as if she had never been asked that question before. Her straight black hair fell over one eye.

"I'm Bree," she said finally in a soft, velvety voice.

"Hi, Bree," Bobby replied, stepping close, his eyes locked on hers. "I'm Bobby Newkirk."

"I know," she said shyly. She brushed the hair away from her face.

"Did you find Mr. Cotton?" he asked.

She nodded. "Yeah. My sister and I wanted to ask him about chorus. I mean, it's kind of late in the year. But we thought maybe we could join. In time for the spring concert."

She sighed, as if explaining all that was a chore.

"You sing?" Bobby asked, studying her face. He liked her green eyes, liked the pale gloss she had on her full lips.

"Well, Samantha and I think so. But I'm not sure

what Mr. Cotton thinks." She smiled for the first time, a brief smile. Then she shyly looked away.

"I'm in a band," Bobby told her. "Did you hear us? I mean, out in the hall?"

She nodded. "A little."

"We could use a singer," Bobby told her. The idea had just popped into his head. "I'm a great guitar player. And I sing okay too. But we could use a girl singer. Maybe you or your sister—?"

"Samantha might like that," Bree replied thoughtfully. "Her voice is a lot stronger than mine." She hesitated, moving a step and staring down into the open locker. "I don't think I could sing rock music."

"You're quiet, huh?" Bobby asked.

Pink circles formed on her pale cheeks.

"Quiet like a mouse?" Bobby teased.

She giggled. "Not *that* quiet." Her hair fell over her eye again. She made no attempt to smooth it away.

"Our band is playing at a club Friday night," Bobby told her. "It's a dance club for teenagers. On Old Mill Road. You know it? It's called The Mill."

Bree shook her head. "No. We just moved here last year. I haven't been—"

"You busy Friday night? Want to come hear us?" Bobby asked.

He could see surprise in her eyes. The pink circles on her cheeks grew darker. "Well—"

"We wouldn't have to stay at the club if you don't like it," he added quickly. "My band is doing just one set. We could leave right after. You know. Go somewhere else."

She raised her eyes to his and stared hard at him as

if trying to read his thoughts. "Okay," she said. "Sounds like fun."

"Way cool," Bobby replied. He stepped back as she turned to pull her backpack out of the locker.

"Know where I live?" she asked. "It's on Fear Street. Way at the end."

"I'll find it," Bobby told her. "See you Friday. About seven-thirty."

He flashed her his most winning smile, then took off for his locker. He knew she was watching him, admiring his walk.

Piece of cake, he thought, very pleased with himself. That was almost too easy.

She's really shy, he decided. But I could see how excited she was that I asked her out.

"One down," he murmured to himself, "and one to go."

"Way to go, man!" Arnie slapped Bobby an enthusiastic high-five.

Bobby did an exaggerated strut around his bedroom. "I'm cool, I'm cool!" he chanted.

"So which one did you get a date with?" Arnie asked.

"Bree," Bobby told him. "Rhymes with *me*. Bree and me!"

"What rhymes with Samantha?" Arnie demanded. "Pink pantha?"

As usual, Bobby didn't laugh at his friend's lame joke. "I'm cool. I'm cool!" He did a little more strutting around his bedroom.

Arnie had stopped by after dinner, as he often did, mainly to avoid doing his homework. Bobby had immediately told him that he'd already asked Bree Wade out that afternoon and, of course, she'd said yes.

"They just can't say no to Bobby the Man!" he cried. He slapped Arnie another high-five. "Who's the Man, Arnie? Who's the Man?"

"You the Man!" Arnie obediently replied. He dropped on top of Bobby's red and white bedspread, sprawling on his back, resting his head in his hands. "What about her sister?"

"I'm calling her right now," Bobby said. "I'm glad you came by, man. You can listen. You can be a witness as I make history!"

Arnie laughed. He was enjoying this as much as Bobby.

Arnie is my biggest fan, Bobby realized. That's why we're such good friends.

"You're really going to ask Samantha out for Saturday night?" Arnie asked, sitting up and stretching his arms up over his head.

Bobby nodded, grinning as he reached for the cordless phone.

"And you're going to tell her not to tell Bree?" Arnie dropped onto his back again.

Bobby nodded again. He searched for the Wades' phone number in the Shadyside High directory he kept by the phone. "Two Wades in one weekend," he muttered, moving his finger down the column of names and numbers. "That's the challenge. And I accept the challenge."

"You the Man!" Arnie proclaimed. "You the Man!"

Bobby punched in the number, then pressed the phone to his ear.

"What if Bree answers?" Arnie demanded. "What if Bree answers and you think it's Samantha?"

"Hey, I can tell them apart," Bobby declared. He raised a finger to his lips, signaling Arnie to be silent.

The phone rang twice. Then a girl's voice on the other end said hello.

Bobby cleared his throat. "Hello—Samantha?"

chapter

5

"Do You Think I'd Do That to My Sister?"

"Yes, this is Samantha. Who's this?"

"Hi, Samantha. It's Bobby Newkirk."

"Oh. Hi!" She sounded very surprised. "Bree and I were just talking about you."

Bobby's smile faded. "Oh. Is she there? In the room with you?"

"No. Bree is downstairs. Want me to get her?"

"No!" Bobby replied quickly. "I wanted to talk to *you*, actually."

"Me?" Her voice wasn't soft and velvety like Bree's. Samantha spoke loudly, Bobby knew.

"Bree said you might be interested in singing with our band," Bobby said, smiling over at Arnie.

Arnie, sprawled on his back on the bed, flashed him an a-okay sign for encouragement.

Samantha laughed scornfully. "Me? Sing with a band? You're kidding!"

"Want to try?" Bobby asked.

"No way!" Samantha cried. "Why would Bree *say* that?"

Bobby chuckled. "I don't know. But that's what she told me."

"Weird," Samantha said. "Well—no thanks. I sound good only in a big group. Or in the shower."

They both laughed.

Arnie sat up, listening intently to Bobby's side of the conversation.

"You busy Saturday night?" Bobby asked casually.

Silence at the other end. He could imagine the stunned expression on her face.

"Want to go to a movie? You know. At the Tenplex?"

More silence. Then finally, Samantha replied in a hushed tone just above a whisper. "But, Bobby, you asked my sister out for the night before."

"Yeah, I know," Bobby replied.

He could hear her short, rapid breathing on the other end. He knew she expected him to say more. So he didn't.

"I don't think Bree would like it if I went out with you the next night," Samantha said, speaking thoughtfully.

"She doesn't have to know about it," Bobby suggested, his voice steady and low. He listened to her breathing, trying to determine what her reaction was.

"Is this a dare or a bet or something?" she demanded angrily. "Did someone dare you to go out with us both? Is that it?"

"No. No way!" Bobby insisted. "I've been thinking

about you. I mean, I see you in homeroom, and I thought—"

"It's not a dare?" she demanded suspiciously.

"No. No way. I swear, Samantha."

A long silence. Bobby waited patiently, his eyes on Arnie.

She's going to say yes, he told himself. She's hot for me and she knows it. She is *stoked*. She's no different from all the other girls at school. She wants to go out with Bobby the Man.

"Bobby," she said finally, "do you really think I'd do that to my sister?"

"Sure you would," Bobby urged. "Sure you would. You *know* you're dying to go out with me—right?"

"You're really conceited," she replied.

"Yeah, I know," Bobby told her. "It's my best quality."

Samantha laughed appreciatively. "I *like* conceited guys!" she declared.

I've *got* her! Bobby told himself gleefully.

"So you'll go out with me Saturday night?" he urged.

"Yeah. Okay," she replied. "To the movies, right?"

"Right," Bobby said, flashing Arnie a two-fingered victory sign. "And it'll be our secret? I mean, your sister—"

"What she doesn't know won't hurt her—much," Samantha said.

It struck Bobby as an odd thing to say. He didn't quite get her meaning. He decided to let it pass. "Maybe we'd better meet at the mall," he told her. "So Bree won't know."

"Good thinking, Ace," Samantha replied. "And we can wear masks so no one will recognize us."

Bobby laughed. "That was a joke, right?" She had such a deadpan delivery, it was hard to tell if she was joking or not.

"Yeah. A joke," she replied dryly. "Uh-oh. I think I hear Bree. I've got to go."

"Meet you Saturday at eight," Bobby said quickly.

"Bye," she whispered. A sexy whisper.

The line went dead.

Bobby tossed the cordless phone into the air. It landed softly on the plush carpet. He turned to Arnie, a triumphant grin on his face. Then he began to do his strut step around the room in celebration.

"I wish I was double-jointed so I could pat myself on the back!" he cried.

"You did it!" Arnie cried. "I don't believe it! You did it! This is the coolest thing I ever heard of!"

"Yeah, it is, isn't it!" Bobby agreed.

He and Arnie did some more celebrating, the two of them strutting around the room, shouting and whooping.

Finally Arnie stopped, a thoughtful expression on his face. He scratched the line of fuzz above his upper lip. It was always itching him. "Samantha isn't going to tell her sister?" he asked.

Bobby shook his head. "It didn't seem to be a problem for her at all." He grinned. "Samantha seems really cool. I mean *really* cool!"

"Wow," Arnie murmured. "Wow." And then he added, "I wonder why Melanie was so bent out of shape about this."

Bobby shrugged. "Who knows? Melanie is weird. I warned you, man."

Arnie shook his head. "But why did she think it was so important to warn you not to go out with the Wade twins?" he demanded.

"I don't know *what* Melanie's problem is," Bobby replied. "I really don't. I mean, what could happen, man? What could happen?"

chapter

6

First Shock

Bree looked awesome, Bobby thought. She wore a short black skirt over red tights and a silky, sleeveless red T-shirt. She had tied her black hair back with a red ribbon. But it had come loose soon after they arrived at The Mill. Now it flowed down past her shoulders, waving behind her as she clapped and swayed to the music.

Bobby watched Bree from the small stage as his fingers moved through the opening notes of "That'll Be the Day." Through the flashing red and blue lights, he could see her standing alone near the back of the dance floor, clapping to the beat.

What an excellent sound system! Bobby thought. He smiled at Paul and Arnie as their music flowed out over the crowded, throbbing dance floor. We sound *great!*

Bobby began to do his Chuck Berry strut. His hands moved automatically. The music flowed through him, around him, *inside* him.

26

The set ended too quickly. Bobby wanted the quaking, shaking blur of throbbing sound and flashing lights, dancing bodies, shouts, and cheers to go on forever.

"They love us!" Bobby cried as he stepped off the stage. "They love us!"

The cheers faded as the deejay turned the music up. The lights continued to flash. Red and blue, red and blue. Bobby pushed through the jumble of twisting, bobbing bodies and shadows to the back of the dance floor, where Bree waited for him.

"How was it?" he shouted. He grabbed a used napkin from a table and mopped the sweat off his forehead.

"What?" Bree shouted.

He leaned closer and shouted over the music, "How was it?"

She smiled. "Great!" Her tiny voice barely rose over the vibrating bass, the steady thud of synthesized drums.

"It's too loud to talk!" Bobby shouted into her ear. "Let's just dance."

They danced for a few songs. Bree, he saw, was too self-conscious to be a good dancer. She can't let go and just dance, he realized. He could see the concentration on her face as she struggled to keep the beat.

"Could we go somewhere and get some fresh air?" she pleaded as the second dance number led into the third. She pushed her dark hair off her shoulders, then grabbed his hand in both of hers and tugged him away. Her hands were hot and wet.

Near the exit they ran into Paul. He had his keyboard under his arm and was heading out.

"We were great! We were awesome! Rock 'n' roll!" Bobby cried, slapping him on the back.

Paul smiled halfheartedly. "We were doing okay, Bobby, until you pulled your amp cord out. Why did you decide to start strutting and dancing around like that?"

"Show biz, man!" Bobby cried. "Show biz. You've got to put on a show for them! Rock 'n' roll, man! They loved us! Did you see their faces? They loved us!"

Paul shook his head. "But you were taking away from us, man! We looked like your backup group."

"They loved us!" Bobby repeated. "They ate it up!"

"Later," Paul said. He smiled at Bree, then pushed open the door and disappeared.

Bobby realized he was still holding Bree's hand. It felt tiny and soft inside his. He leaned close to her so he could smell her hair. It smelled like coconut.

She's really great looking, he told himself. A lot of guys are staring at me. They're jealous because I'm with her and they're not. Too bad she can't dance. And too bad she's so shy. She barely said two words when we drove to the club.

Bobby glanced back at the dance floor, flooded in swirling red lights. Arnie was dancing with Melanie. Bobby gave Arnie a wave and a shout, but Arnie couldn't see him.

Melanie looks really chubby in those shorts, Bobby thought nastily. Hope she doesn't split them open. Actually, I hope she does!

When he had entered the club earlier, Melanie had greeted Bree warmly and deliberately snubbed Bobby.

As if I care, he thought.

Why did I ever date her? he asked himself.

Oh, well, I've learned my lesson. No more charity cases.

"Let's get out of here," he told Bree. "We'll get that fresh air you wanted."

He led the way out to the parking lot.

It was a clear night, cold for April, more like winter than spring. The stars shimmered in the purple night sky.

Bree shivered as she lowered herself into the passenger seat of his red Bonneville. "I should've brought a sweater or something," she murmured.

He shut the door. I'll bet I could warm you up real fast, he said to himself.

They cruised around Shadyside for a while. He slipped a CD into the player and turned it up. Classical guitar music. That always impressed girls, he knew.

He had to do most of the talking. He talked about the band, about his classes, about the summer vacation in Hawaii his family was planning to take when he got home from working as a camp counselor in Massachusetts.

He wished she weren't so shy and quiet. And he wished she wouldn't cling to the passenger door as if she might jump out at any moment.

"You're the one with the monkeys, right?" she said as they drove by Shadyside High, now dark and empty. "I mean, your science project?"

"Wayne and Garth? Yeah, they're mine." He drove with one hand, his right hand on the gearshift, even

29

though the car was an automatic. "It's a diet experiment. I'm feeding Wayne only bananas and water. Garth is getting a mixed diet."

"Where on earth did you get the monkeys?" she asked.

"My uncle," Bobby told her. "He's an animal importer. He works for zoos. They're great monkeys, but I can't keep them. I have to send them back when the experiment is over."

"It's a neat experiment," Bree said, settling back in the seat.

"I don't think Mr. Conklin appreciates it," Bobby told her.

She turned to him. "Why not?"

"Because the monkeys look so much like him!"

They both laughed. Her laugh sounded more like coughing than laughing, Bobby thought.

"Do you take them home on weekends?" she asked.

He shook his head. "No. Conklin does."

He kept glancing at her as he drove, trying to decide if she liked him or not. Of *course* she likes me, he told himself. But does she *really* like me?

As he drove, he had a fantasy of the Wade twins fighting over him. They were wrestling on the ground, tearing and scratching at each other, each desperate to have him for herself.

Did he like her? he wondered. Of course he did. She was a *babe,* wasn't she?

At a little before twelve, he pulled up her driveway and switched off the engine and the lights. He turned to talk to her.

But she startled him by nearly jumping into his lap.

"I had a nice time," she whispered. Before Bobby

could reply, she grabbed his head with both hands, pressed her face against his, and kissed him longingly.

The kiss lasted a long time.

Then, uttering a soft sigh, she raised her face to his and kissed him again, harder this time, and longer.

I don't believe this! Bobby thought. She's nuts about me!

She wrapped her hot hands around his neck and held his face close as she kissed him again. When it ended, they were both breathless.

"I've got to go in," she whispered. She pressed her forehead against his. Her hair brushed his face. "Want to come over tomorrow night? We could watch a video or something."

The question caught Bobby by surprise. He almost blurted out, No, I can't. I have a date with your sister tomorrow.

But he caught himself, and replied, "I wish I could, Bree. I really do. But I'm—busy."

Her lips formed an unhappy pout. She brushed them against his cheek as she pulled away from him. "Good night," she whispered. "Call me, okay?"

He watched her jog to the back of the house. He could still taste her lips on his, still feel the warm tingle of her hands on the back of his neck.

Wow, he thought. You never can tell with the quiet ones!

As he backed down the driveway, he couldn't help but grin to himself. "Bobby the Man scores again!" he cried out loud.

If *she's* the shy one, I can't *wait* to check out her sister!

* * *

Bobby waited for Samantha the next night in the food court at the Division Street Mall. She arrived a few minutes late, jogging toward Bobby, her black hair flowing wildly behind her.

She wore loose-fitting faded denim shorts and a bright magenta midriff blouse.

Oh, wow! Is she *sexy!* Bobby played it cool and forced her to come all the way to him. His first impulse was to tell her she looked incredible. But instead he murmured in a low voice, "Hey, how's it going?"

She didn't reply. Instead, she took his arm and pulled him toward the wall. "We can't do this, Bobby," she said in a low, frightened voice.

"Huh?" he reacted with surprise.

"We can't meet like this," she told him. Her eyes darted nervously around the crowded court. "Look! There's Bree!"

chapter

7

First Danger Sign

"**H**uh? Where?" Bobby cried.

As his eyes searched the crowd, he took a moment to realize that Samantha was laughing.

"Gotcha," she murmured, taking his arm. Her green eyes stared triumphantly into his.

"No way. I didn't believe you," Bobby insisted.

"Then what was that terrified expression on your face?" she demanded. "You looked like you were going to swallow your tongue!"

"No way!" he protested, laughing.

"Well, I feel like we're in a spy movie or something," she confided in a low voice. "What if someone does see us?"

Bobby shrugged. "No problem," he replied casually. She had thrown him off with her phony scare. Now he had to be extra cool, he decided, to impress her.

"Did you bring the plans, Boris?" she whispered. "Do you know the password?"

He snickered. "You're weird."

Her expression turned serious again. Still holding his arm, she raised her green eyes to his. "I just feel a little strange sneaking around like this, Bobby. I mean, Bree told me she had a great time last night. I think she really likes you."

"Hey, I'm a likable guy," Bobby boasted, flashing her his best smile. He checked out his reflection in a window and pushed back his blond hair.

"So it's not nice of me to go out with you tonight, is it?" Samantha asked, staring into his eyes.

"Well . . ." Bobby couldn't think of a good answer.

She answered before he could say anything. "Who wants to be *nice?*" she exclaimed. "Nice is boring!"

They both laughed.

She is *hot!* Bobby thought, trying to be cool and not stare at the bare skin below her midriff top. She's not like her sister at all, he decided.

"I—noticed you in homeroom," Samantha said, following him to the ticket booth.

"Hey, I noticed you too," Bobby replied with a meaningful smirk. "I mean, who wouldn't?"

She giggled.

She likes to be flattered, he decided.

"You've got quite a reputation," she said.

He stopped walking. He wasn't used to girls being so direct. She says whatever she thinks, he realized.

"I mean, girls at school, they talk about you," Samantha confided.

"Yeah? What do they say?" Bobby demanded.

She flashed him a smile. "I'm not telling," she replied coyly. "You're already too conceited."

"Well, whatever you heard, it's probably true," he said.

34

She laughed again. Her laugh was loud and throaty, he noticed. Not like Bree's quiet, coughing one.

She has a lot more personality than Bree, Bobby decided. And it's obvious she's really *stoked* for Bobby the Man.

They stopped in front of the ticket booth. "What movie do you want to see?" Bobby asked. *"Eradicator Five?* The special effects are supposed to be outstanding!"

"Those films are gross," Samantha replied. She grinned, then added, "I love them!"

"So you want to see it?"

She frowned and pulled her hair back with both hands. "I saw it already. Do we have to go to a movie? Can't we just hang out?"

"Yeah. No problem," Bobby quickly agreed.

She probably just wants to drive up to River Ridge and make out, he told himself. This one doesn't want to waste any time.

"I like walking around the mall," she said as they started away from the movie theater. "You see so many cool things."

"You like to shop?" he asked.

"No. Bree is the shopper. I just like to look." They entered the mall and walked for a while, stopping to gaze into store windows.

In front of the Gold Barn, a jewelry store, she turned to him, a devilish expression on her face. "Bree would kill me if she knew I was here with you," she confided.

"She won't find out," Bobby replied, checking out his reflection in the display window.

"Did you have a good time with Bree last night?" Samantha demanded.

Before he could reply, she laughed and pointed across the aisle. "Look at those people! Do you *believe* them!" she cried scornfully. "They're eating hot dogs, nachos, and ice cream all at the same time. Think they know the way to the food court?"

"Fat chance," Bobby joked. "Uh-oh," he said quickly, "I'm starting to sound like Arnie!"

"Arnie? Melanie's boyfriend?" Samantha asked.

"Yeah. He's my best friend," Bobby told her.

"Weird," she replied.

He didn't understand her reaction. But he didn't have time to question her. She pulled him into the Gold Barn.

"I thought you didn't like to shop," he protested.

"I don't. But I *love* earrings!" she exclaimed. She dangled the two large gold hoops from her ears "See?" Then she turned to the wall of earrings.

Bobby glanced back through the small store. It was long and narrow with a display counter across the back and walls of earrings on both sides.

"My cousin worked here one summer," he told Samantha. "The owners know me."

"Thrills and chills," she commented sarcastically. She handed him the gold hoops. Then she playfully pushed him out of the way to try on a long, dangly pair of silver earrings.

"Help me with these," she said, holding her hair back with one hand to insert the earring in her pierced ear. "Oh, wait. I like those better."

She reached for another pair and held them up to him. "Look, Bobby. Silver fish. Aren't they great?"

He nodded.

"Which do you like better—the dangly ones or the fish? Oh, never mind. I'll try them both."

As she tried on the first pair, Bobby turned to the display counter in back. He didn't recognize any of the salespeople.

His eye fell on the large sign in the center of the wall. In bold red type it declared: SHOPLIFTERS WILL BE ARRESTED AND PROSECUTED TO THE FULL EXTENT OF THE LAW.

He juggled the two gold hoops in his hand. They looked like solid gold. But they were actually hollow and light.

"Excuse me, miss," a saleslady called out from across the store. Samantha was reaching for a pair of delicate gold heart-shaped earrings. "It is against store policy to let customers try on pierced earrings. Please don't put on any more."

"Sure, no problem," Samantha said with a smile. "Aren't these great?" she asked.

"Great," Bobby replied without enthusiasm.

"I could shop for earrings all night," she told him.

"Wow. This *is* going to be an exciting night!" he teased, rolling his eyes.

She turned to him, her eyes lighting up. "You want excitement?" She seemed to be challenging him.

He grinned. "You know my reputation," he boasted. "I'm always pumped for a little excitement."

"Okay," she said, grinning back. "Let's go." She started to the door.

"Hey, wait!" Bobby hurried after her. "Your earrings!"

Samantha didn't look back. Walking with quick,

steady strides, she continued toward the open doorway.

Bobby ran to catch up with her. He had her gold hoops in one hand. He grabbed her shoulder with the other. "Those heart earrings—you didn't pay for them."

He glanced back at the salespeople behind the counter in the back. Were they watching?

"I know I didn't pay for them," Samantha whispered, shoving her earrings into her pocketbook. "Let's go."

"What are you doing?" Bobby demanded.

"I'm taking a hundred percent discount," she said casually.

As they stepped into the doorway, they heard a loud, urgent call from the back of the store: "Young lady—stop! Young lady!"

Bobby hesitated. But Samantha grabbed his hand and tugged on it.

"Young lady! Stop! Stop!"

Bobby glanced back to see two salespeople racing toward them.

Samantha pulled him out the door. "Bobby, *run!*" she cried.

chapter

8

Caught

"*R*un!" Samantha screamed.

She let go of Bobby's hand and darted into the crowded mall.

Bobby uttered a single gasp, then took off after her.

"Stop them!"

"Hey—stop!"

Angry shouts rose over the voices of the crowd. Glancing back over his shoulder, Bobby saw a middle-aged man and a young woman running full-speed after them.

"Look out!"

Bobby nearly collided with a wide double stroller with two sleeping toddlers. He stopped short, dodging to his left.

"Watch where you're going!" the woman behind the stroller snapped.

"Sorry!" Bobby called back, and started running again.

39

He lost Samantha for a moment, then spotted her magenta top in a crowd in front of a CD store.

"Stop them! Hey—stop them!" The two salespeople were still in pursuit.

"Samantha!" Bobby called breathlessly.

She didn't seem to hear. He watched her disappear around a corner.

Bobby stopped short to avoid stumbling over two little girls carrying ice-cream cones. Then he plunged around the corner.

He felt a sharp stab of pain in his side as he caught up with Samantha. "Ow. Wait up!"

To his surprise, she was laughing. Laughing excitedly, gleefully.

They cut across the near end of the food court, ducked through a line at the McDonald's, ran between two rows of yellow plastic tables.

The pain in Bobby's side grew sharper. He took a deep breath and tried to *will* it away.

"Whoa—Samantha! Wait!"

Past a Gap store. Then a Waldenbooks.

The pain in his side faded. He was breathing hard. Running fast. Right behind her now.

Her black hair flew out behind her like a pennant on a windy day. He caught up, passed her, saw her green eyes glowing with excitement. She was still laughing.

He glanced behind them. No sign of the salespeople.

Had he and Samantha managed to lose them? Had they gotten away safely?

"Whoa! Samantha—why?" he asked breathlessly. "Why'd you do it?"

"For fun!" she shouted.

She kept running, her dark hair flying behind her, and he ran with her.

People backed out of their way. Bobby ignored their angry, surprised shouts.

They turned a corner past a doughnut shop. They darted in front of a group of teenagers heading into Pete's Pizza.

Bobby gasped as a gray-uniformed security guard stepped forward. The man blocked their path, his eyes narrowed in anger.

"Oh, no. We're caught!" Bobby murmured aloud.

chapter

9

"Don't Hurt Her"

*B*obby stopped so quickly, he bumped into Samantha. He was breathing hard, and his side ached again. Then he realized he still had the two gold hoops in his fist.

"Not so fast," the security guard said. He pushed his gray cap back on his head and stared from one to the other with bloodshot eyes.

Caught, Bobby thought. We're caught.

Of all the dumb stunts, he told himself, still struggling to catch his breath. Why did Samantha do that? And why did she drag me into it?

"What's your hurry?" the guard asked in a slow drawl.

"We-we're late," Samantha managed to stammer.

Pretty lame, Bobby thought.

The guard narrowed his eyes at Samantha.

Bobby squeezed the gold hoops in his fist. He saw that Samantha's hair was hanging around her face.

He heard shouting behind him. The salespeople from the Gold Barn?

He glanced back to see. No. Just a bickering middle-aged couple.

Then he turned back to face the stern security guard. Would Samantha confess she had taken the earrings? he wondered. Did she have an excuse ready for the guard?

"You really shouldn't run," the guard told them. "You could get hurt."

"Sorry," Samantha told him, lowering her eyes.

"These floors can be slippery," the guard warned. "So take it easy, hear?"

"Yes, we will," Samantha said solemnly. "Sorry."

The guard made a gesture with one hand, dismissing them. "Young people. Always in a hurry," he muttered to himself as he turned and headed off.

Bobby and Samantha managed to keep straight faces until they reached the parking garage. Then they fell apart, laughing and congratulating each other, howling jubilantly over their close call.

"That was *outstanding!*" Samantha declared gleefully. *"Outstanding!"*

Secretly, Bobby didn't think the earrings were worth the risk Samantha had taken. His heart was still racing, and he felt shaky. But he didn't want to look like a wimp. "Hey, that was better than a movie!" he told her.

"Those floors can be slippery. So take it easy." Samantha did a pretty good imitation of the guard's slow drawl.

They both burst out laughing again. Bobby slapped her a high-five.

"When that guard stopped us, I nearly had a cow!" Bobby admitted.

"He was old. We could've taken him," Samantha replied casually.

Bobby stared at her. What did she mean by that? Was she just joking?

"Let's get out of here!" she cried, her eyes flashing with excitement.

They jogged across the garage to his red Bonneville, their sneakers loud on the concrete.

"I'll drive!" Samantha cried breathlessly. She held out her hand for Bobby's car keys.

He hesitated.

"I want to drive!" she insisted. She grabbed the keys from his hand.

"Used to getting your way a lot?" he teased.

"Always!" she replied. She dropped into the driver seat and had the car started and the lights on before Bobby had opened his door. The engine roared as she pressed her foot down all the way on the gas pedal.

"Are you used to a V-six?" Bobby asked warily. "This car has a lot of pickup."

She squeezed his hand. "I can handle it," she replied dryly.

Bobby grabbed the door handle as she backed out of the parking space without looking. The tires squealed as she went forward and roared around the corner toward the exit.

She bolted through the exit without slowing to turn into the traffic on Division Street. She ignored the honking horns.

Bobby swallowed hard and slumped low in the passenger seat.

Samantha tossed her head back, laughing loudly.

"What's so funny?" Bobby demanded as she cut off a pizza van to get into the middle lane.

"The look on your face," she replied. "Don't worry, Bobby. I'm a good driver." She cut back into the right lane. More horns honked angrily behind them.

Bobby glanced at the speedometer. She was going too fast.

He started to tell her to slow down, but stopped himself. He was supposed to be cool, he told himself. So how cool would it be to scold her for driving too fast?

"I love speed, don't you?" she asked, making a sharp, squealing turn onto River Road. "I love going fast! It gets me so—pumped." She glanced at him coyly.

"Me too," Bobby replied, trying to sound as if he meant it. "Where are we going?"

"You'll see." She rolled down her window. The cool wind made her hair flutter wildly behind her. "This is great! This is *great!*" she cried, shouting over the roar of the wind.

Houses with streetlights gave way to dark woods. They were driving along the river now, Bobby knew. He saw Samantha floor the gas pedal as the road began to climb to the rock cliffs that overlooked the riverbank.

I don't *believe* this! he thought. Is she driving to River Ridge?

River Ridge, the high cliff overlooking the Conononka River and the town, was the big makeout spot for Shadyside teenagers.

Wow! She doesn't waste any time! Bobby thought happily.

Finally she slowed the car as they reached the top. She guided it past a couple of parked cars and pulled to a stop at the cliff edge beside a clump of tall shrubs.

Samantha cut the engine and the lights, then pulled her disheveled hair back with both hands. "Well, look where we are," she whispered, staring out through the windshield.

"Nice driving," Bobby said with a grin.

"You haven't been up here before, have you?" she teased.

"Maybe a few times," he replied, leaning toward her.

"I think I like you," she murmured.

As they kissed, he wrapped his arms around her shoulders. The kiss lasted a long time.

I don't *believe* these twins! Bobby thought. He remembered Bree's kisses, so hungry, so *needy*.

I can't *wait* to tell Arnie! Bobby thought as they stopped to catch their breath. Arnie will totally freak out!

He kissed her again. Bobby the Man will be the talk of Shadyside High on Monday! he told himself. No one will believe I made out with *both* Wade twins in one weekend!

What was it Samantha had said to him when they met at the mall? "You have quite a reputation." Yeah. That's what she said.

Well, you ain't seen nothin' yet! Bobby thought.

When word gets out about this weekend—the all-

Wade weekend!—everyone will know who's the coolest guy in school!

I am the king! Bobby thought, kissing her again.

The king of rock 'n' roll!

Samantha pulled back and stared at him, her eyes half shut. "I told you I like to go fast," she whispered.

Bobby settled back in the passenger seat. This girl was just so *hot*, so *hot!* He wondered if it would be too late to call Arnie that night.

"What are you thinking about?" Samantha demanded dreamily.

"I'm just thinking how great you are," Bobby lied.

Smooth. Very smooth, he congratulated himself.

She opened her eyes wide. "Do you like me better than Bree?"

The blunt question startled him. "Yeah. Sure, I do."

She smiled. The wind fluttered her hair. She settled back on the car seat and stared out the windshield.

Bobby followed her gaze. The black sky was dotted with a million tiny white stars. A hazy sliver of cloud cut the pale full moon in half.

"I'm a little different from my sister," Samantha said softly, staring up at the sky.

"Yeah," Bobby agreed. Then he added, "But you two *look* so much alike. You really do. How do people tell you apart?"

Samantha turned to him with a sly smile. "There's a way to tell us apart," she said coyly.

"How?" Bobby demanded.

She brought her face close to his and whispered in his ear, "When we get to know each other better, I'll show you." Her soft breath tickled his ear, made a chill run down the back of his neck.

47

Wow, he thought. Wow.

"I think Bree really likes you," she told him, her smile fading.

"I think I like you better," Bobby replied.

"You'd better be careful," she said, avoiding his eyes.

"Huh? What do you mean?"

"Well . . ." She hesitated. "Bree is kind of fragile."

"Fragile?"

"You'd better be careful not to hurt her," Samantha warned, raising her eyes to Bobby's. "Bree can be a little—strange when she's hurt."

Bobby stared hard at Samantha. A cloud drifted over the moon, and her face darkened. "Samantha, what do you mean?" he asked.

"I really don't want to talk about it," she told him. Her eyes narrowed. "Just be careful with Bree, Bobby. Be very careful."

chapter

10

Three's a Crowd

*B*obby slammed his locker shut and headed down the hall. The final bell had rung. The school was emptying quickly.

A riff from an old Chuck Berry song kept repeating in his head. As he made his way to the music room, he was thinking about trying it on the guitar.

The band was really starting to *cook*, Bobby thought, waving to some kids heading out the door. Bright afternoon sunlight burst into the hall as they pushed the double doors open.

Too bad Paul was threatening to quit. Just when they were starting to play so well together. Paul had given an excuse about having to get an after-school job.

But Bobby thought he knew the real reason—Paul was jealous of him. He's a good, dependable player. But he doesn't have my style, and he knows it.

Turning a corner, waving to a group of girls from his

49

class, he decided to have a talk with Paul. I'll tell him how much we need him, Bobby decided. I'll make him think he's the leader, make him feel like a big man. He'll stay.

Spotting Kimmy Bass at her locker, Bobby crept up behind her and gave her hair a hard tug.

Kimmy shrieked angrily and spun around. "Bobby —you creep!" She sneered at him. "Get your disgusting paws off me!"

"You love it!" Bobby shot back, grinning.

"Creep," Kimmy repeated in a low voice.

"Are you doing anything Saturday night?" Bobby asked her.

She stared at him suspiciously. "Why?"

"Just asking," Bobby said, his blue eyes returning the stare.

"No, I'm not doing anything," Kimmy told him.

"Then why not take a bath?" Bobby let out a high-pitched hyena laugh.

"Aaaaagh!" Kimmy let out a disgusted cry and punched him in the chest. "You really are a pig, Bobby!"

"Oink-oink. Takes one to know one." He backed away from another flying fist, and chuckling to himself, hurried down the hall.

She's nuts about me, he told himself confidently. Totally nuts about me.

But I don't have time for her now. I've got enough to handle. Twins!

Arnie and Melanie were standing by the music room window, talking quietly. Paul was noodling at his keyboard. "Hey—what's up?" Bobby called.

Arnie called out a greeting. But Melanie only acted

disgusted, narrowing her dark eyes and then turning toward the window.

"I *see* you're having a bad hair day, Melanie. But why take it out on me?" Bobby demanded.

Melanie didn't turn around. She crossed her arms in front of her chest. "Are you still dating both Wade twins?" she asked through clenched teeth.

"Yeah. Maybe," Bobby replied. "What's it to you?"

Melanie didn't reply. Arnie shrugged.

"Are we going to rehearse or not?" Paul called impatiently from behind his keyboard.

Melanie turned to face Bobby, her features tight. "I don't believe you," she said sharply.

Bobby grinned back at her. "I don't believe it either!" he exclaimed. "Two at once. Even *I'm* impressed!"

"When are you *not* impressed with yourself?" Melanie accused.

"Paul's right. We've got to practice," Arnie interrupted.

But Bobby saw that Melanie was determined to have her say. "You had a study date with Samantha the other night and Bree showed up at your house. Is that really true?" she demanded.

Bobby grinned. "I guess people are talking about me, huh?"

"Is it true?" Melanie asked.

Bobby nodded. "Yeah. No problem. Samantha got out the back door just as Bree came into the living room. Bree didn't suspect a thing."

"Close one, man," Arnie murmured, grinning. "Wow."

Melanie flashed Arnie an angry look, then returned

to Bobby. "Everyone in school is talking about it," she told Bobby. "I know you think it's really great. But what makes you think Bree won't find out about you and her sister?"

"Is it *your* problem?" Bobby shot back.

"They're my friends," Melanie replied with emotion.

"Hey—mine too," Bobby replied with a smirk. He grinned at Arnie. "They're wearing me out, man. They're *too much*—even for me!"

Arnie started to laugh, but Melanie's stare made him cut it short.

"I can't believe Bree hasn't figured it out," she told Bobby, shaking her head. "How can you and Samantha *do* that to her?"

Bobby shrugged. "Bree is a big girl. She can take it."

"But, Bobby," Melanie insisted shrilly, "what happens when Bree finds out? She'll be so hurt, feel so betrayed. You could tear their whole family apart."

"That's the breaks," Bobby replied with a shrug. He headed to the cabinet for his guitar.

Bobby studied his face in the dresser mirror. It was a little after nine o'clock, and he still had plenty of homework to do. But it was hard to concentrate.

He had been lying on his bed, his government text open in front of him. But thoughts of Bree and Samantha kept him from reading.

If I had to dump one of them, which one would it be? he asked himself.

They were so alike. Yet so different.

And they both seemed to be totally crazy about him.

He had pulled himself up and walked to the mirror. Brushing his blond hair, he studied his face, his smile.

He liked what he saw.

The phone on the desk rang, interrupting his admiration session. He let it ring a few times. If it was a girl, he didn't want to seem too eager. He finally picked up the receiver and said hello in a low voice.

"Two's company. Three's a crowd," a voice whispered in his ear.

"Huh?" Bobby pulled the receiver from his ear and stared at it as if that would help him recognize the caller. "Hey—who *is* this?" he demanded.

"Two's company. Three's a crowd," the whisperer repeated. *"You'll pay."*

"Huh? What's the joke?" Bobby asked, struggling to hear the words, listening hard for a clue to the caller's identity.

"You'll pay," the voice repeated menacingly. *"You'll pay double."*

chapter

11

The Surprise Visitor

*B*obby gripped the receiver hard, listening to the threat. He had read books and seen movies in which people got scary phone calls. But he never thought it would happen to him.

Who would try to scare me? he asked himself.

Everyone *likes* me!

"Samantha—is that you?" he demanded. "It's you, right?" He knew this was the kind of dumb joke Samantha would pull. She loved to surprise him, to shock him. "Living on the edge," she called it.

He heard a quiet snicker at the other end of the line.

"Whoa! Arnie!" Bobby cried. "Give it up, man. I recognize you now."

The quiet snicker burst into a high-pitched laugh. "How'd you know, man?"

"Arnie, I'd recognize your stupid laugh anywhere," Bobby said, feeling relieved. "What is your problem anyway?"

"Just goofing," Arnie replied. "I thought maybe you

54

needed a little excitement. I mean, your life is so *boring* these days."

"You're jealous. Face it," Bobby said, relaxing his hold on the receiver. He dropped down to sit on the edge of his desk.

"Hey, no way!" Arnie insisted.

"You're jealous because Bobby the Man has got both of the Wade twins and—"

"No way," Arnie repeated. "Why would I be jealous? I know I eventually get your rejects."

Bobby laughed. "Well, you can have Bree when I decide to dump her," he told his friend. "Or maybe Samantha," he added. "Or maybe both."

Arnie laughed. "Wow, Bobby. I don't *believe* you! How long are you going to keep this up? I mean, going out with both of them."

"As long as I can!" Bobby replied. "They're both hot, Arnie. I mean, really *hot!* And they're both stoked about me. But," he added, "what else is new?"

Arnie chuckled. "At least you're not conceited or anything."

"Who? Me?"

They both laughed.

"Melanie is having a cow about this," Arnie said seriously.

Bobby shifted the phone to his other ear. "Yeah, I know. What's her problem, man? She's got *you* now. She isn't still hung up on *me*—is she?"

"No," Arnie replied thoughtfully.

"So why is she on my case?" Bobby demanded. "Why does she care what I do with the Wade twins?"

"You know girls," Arnie answered flatly.

Bobby started to reply with a nasty comment about

Melanie. But the doorbell rang downstairs, interrupting him. He told Arnie goodbye, hung up the phone, and glanced at the clock radio. A little after ten.

Who would be at the door this late?

The bell rang again. And again. Bobby's parents were at a neighbor's. "Give me a break! I'm coming!" Bobby called, hurrying down the stairs two at a time.

He pulled open the front door.

"Bree! What's wrong?" he asked.

She stared at him with troubled eyes. "Bobby," she whispered. "We've got to talk."

chapter

12

Bree Found Out!

"*B*ree—what's up?" Bobby asked. "It's so late and—"

She brushed past him into the house. Her black hair was tied behind her head with a blue band. She wore a pale green polo shirt over baggy faded denim shorts.

She's found out! Bobby realized, a heavy feeling forming in the pit of his stomach.

Bree has found out about Samantha and me.

As he led the way to the den, his mind raced with ideas about how to handle it. I could lie and tell her she's crazy, he told himself. I could tell her I've never been out with her sister.

Or I could just shrug it off and say, "What's the big deal?"

No, wait. I could admit I went out with Samantha —but tell Bree that *she* is my favorite, that *she's* the best.

Yeah, Bobby decided. She'll go for that in a big way. Girls just want to be told that *they're* the best.

She'll eat it up. And then we'll be right back where we were. Everyone all happy and bright eyed again.

Bree dropped down close to Bobby on the leather couch. She tugged nervously at a strand of hair that had fallen loose. Then she clasped her hands tightly in her lap.

"It—it's about Samantha," she stammered, raising her troubled eyes to his.

Uh-oh. Here it comes, Bobby thought. "Samantha?" he said innocently. "What's up with Samantha?"

He held his breath and waited for Bree to accuse him. She's probably going to start bawling, he thought unhappily. I really hate it when girls cry.

"Samantha is—seeing someone," Bree said, her voice just above a whisper.

"Yeah. So?" Bobby asked.

Here it comes. Here it comes.

Here's where she bursts into tears and says, "Bobby, how could you?"

Bree took a deep breath. Her eyes burned into Bobby's as if searching for something. "Samantha has been sneaking out with someone," she told him, clasping and unclasping her hands. "I know she has been."

And do you also know that it's me? Bobby wondered, wishing she would put an end to the suspense.

Let's just get this over with, Bree, he thought.

"Well, why are you so upset?" he asked sympathetically.

"I—I asked Samantha about it," Bree continued,

lowering her gaze. "I asked her who she was seeing, and she wouldn't tell me."

Bobby waited for Bree to continue, but she chewed her bottom lip instead.

Confused, Bobby waited. But when he realized she wasn't going to say any more, he broke the silence. "And that's why you're upset?"

"Well, don't you see?" she asked impatiently. "Don't you understand? Samantha and I—we've always confided in each other. We've always told each other everything. That's what it's like, being twins. It's like we're part of the same person. We're closer than sisters. We're *twin* sisters. We've never had any secrets. Never. We've always told each other *everything.*" She added sadly, "Until now."

She doesn't know! Bobby realized.

She knows Samantha is sneaking out with someone. But she doesn't know it's me!

He settled back on the couch, very relieved. He had to force himself not to laugh, not to break out in a wild dance of celebration.

"I'm so upset," Bree confided, shaking her head. "I had to talk to someone. And you—well, I feel I can tell you things, Bobby."

He slid his arm around her shoulders. He still had a strong urge to burst out laughing. But he held it back and said, "I'm glad you feel that way, Bree. Maybe I can help."

Her eyes opened wide. "Help? How?"

"Well, I've got a lot of friends at school," he replied, pulling her close. "I mean, *everyone* knows me— right? I'll ask around for you. You know, try to find out who this guy is. I'm sure someone will tell me who Samantha's secret boyfriend is."

What a laugh! he thought.

"Oh, Bobby, thanks," Bree said softly. She snuggled her forehead against his cheek. "Thanks, Bobby," she whispered. "I don't know what I'd do without you. You—you've become so—important to me."

"Hey, no problem," Bobby replied softly. He raised her face to his for a long, emotional kiss.

"You have to break up with her right away," Samantha said.

Bobby's mouth dropped open. "Whoa!" he murmured.

"I mean it, Bobby. You have to."

Bree had left five minutes earlier, after telling Bobby how much he meant to her. As soon as he closed the door behind her, Bobby began strutting triumphantly around the house.

"Who's the greatest? Who's the greatest?" he chanted to himself.

It was so easy to control girls, Bobby decided. A piece of cake!

You just had to tell them how great they were and act real sympathetic to every dumb thing they said— and they'd fall all over you.

Of course, it helps to have my good looks, Bobby told himself. And it helps to be rich and drive a cool car.

But you've got to know how to talk to girls, how to make them think you really care about them.

He was still congratulating himself on his performance with Bree when the phone rang. He hurried to the kitchen and grabbed the receiver off the wall.

"Bobby, it's me." Samantha, sounding very upset.

Now what? he thought. "What's up, Sam?"

"Bobby, Bree is on her way to your house. She suspects something," Samantha replied.

"She's already been here," Bobby told her. He stretched the phone cord across the room, opened the refrigerator with one hand, and pulled out a can of Coke.

"She has?" Samantha sounded frightened. "Does she know anything? Does she know about you and me?"

"No way," Bobby replied casually. "I took care of it. No problem." He snapped the can open and took a long slug.

"Really? She doesn't know?"

"I told her I'd try to find out who your secret boyfriend is," Bobby said, snickering.

Silence on Samantha's end. "Bobby, we can't do this anymore. You have to break up with her, right away."

Bobby nearly choked on his drink. He set the can down on the white Formica counter.

"For one thing," Samantha continued without waiting for a reply, "I'm tired of sharing you. Why should I sit home alone on Friday nights while you're out with her?"

Bobby grunted a reply. He was thinking hard, trying to figure out the best way to stall Samantha. He was enjoying going out with both girls. He didn't want to end it with Bree so soon.

"You have to do it right away," Samantha said in a trembling voice. "Bree is very suspicious. She's starting to go over the edge, Bobby. You don't know her. She's fragile—like glass. If she breaks . . ."

"Yeah?" Bobby asked, tilting the can up and taking another long drink.

"If she breaks, she could do *anything,*" Samantha said breathlessly.

"Anything?" Bobby replied.

"Anything," Samantha whispered.

chapter

13

Crime Spree

"Samantha—whoa! Stop!" Bobby screamed.

Samantha tossed her head back, laughing gleefully.

"I mean it!" Bobby cried. "Pull over! Let me drive!"

"No way!" she shouted over the roar of the car engine. Her window was down. The air blew her hair wildly out from her head. Her eyes sparked with excitement.

Houses and trees whirred past in a dark blur. A car horn blared angrily as Samantha spun onto Division Street without checking the oncoming traffic.

"I bet you!" she screamed. "I bet you I can drive to the mall without stopping once!"

"You're crazy!" Bobby told her, shutting his eyes.

Horns honked. Bobby thought he heard a police siren start up behind them.

"My car!" he cried. "You're going to wreck my car!"

She laughed and swerved into the left lane, cutting

off an enormous truck. She swept a hand back through her wild, tangled hair.

"Please!" Bobby begged.

"I love it when you're frightened!" she cried, pressing her foot harder on the gas pedal. The red Bonneville shot forward, bursting up to a stop sign. Bobby heard a squeal of tires as a car in the intersection swerved to avoid them.

"I thought you were supposed to be so cool!" Samantha taunted him, her eyes glowing excitedly.

"You—you're crazy!" he cried.

She hit the brake hard to turn into the mall. The car nearly spun all the way around. Bobby heard another car squeal to a stop. Horns blared.

Samantha tossed her head back again in triumphant laughter. "We made it! All the way without stopping! I win the bet!"

Bobby swallowed hard. His heart felt as if it were clogging his throat. His stomach was knotted into a hard, tight rock.

Her windblown hair wild about her face, Samantha pulled Bobby's car into a narrow parking space and cut the engine. She turned to him and grinned. "Well? Are you impressed?"

Bobby uttered an angry cry. "What if we had crashed into something?" he demanded shrilly. "What if the police had stopped us? Do you have any idea of how much trouble you'd be in? They'd take your driver's license away!"

"No, they wouldn't," Samantha assured him calmly, pushing open the car door. "I don't have a driver's license."

* * *

Bobby calmed down a bit as he and Samantha made their usual Saturday night tour of the mall. He realized he had blown his image by shrieking at her in the car.

But he didn't care. After all, it *was* his car she was trying to wreck, he decided. And she could've easily gotten them both killed.

Didn't she care about her own life? he wondered. Was excitement so important to Samantha that she'd risk her life—and his—to get it?

Heavy thoughts, Bobby told himself.

She's just totally nuts, he decided. Maybe I should break up with Samantha and keep going with Bree. It would certainly be a lot safer.

"Did you break up with Bree last night?" Samantha asked as if reading his thoughts.

The question caught him by surprise. "Uh—well . . ."

They were sitting across from each other in a red vinyl booth at Pete's Pizza. The waitress had just set a pie down on their table, and Bobby was reaching for a slice.

Samantha liked peppers, mushrooms, onions, and pepperoni on her pizza. Bobby liked his plain. So they had ordered the pizza half and half.

She's even weird about pizza, Bobby thought, studying her as she picked the mushroom pieces off her slice and popped them into her mouth.

"Bree said you took her to a party at Suki Thomas's," Samantha said, dabbing the top of her pizza slice with a napkin to soak up the excess oil.

"Yeah," Bobby mumbled, lowering his eyes. "Suki's parents were out of town, so she had a party."

"You didn't have a serious talk with Bree?" Samantha demanded. "You didn't tell her you weren't going to see her anymore?" She took a large bite of pizza. "Ow! Hot!"

"I always burn my mouth on the first bite," Bobby said, eager to change the subject. "Always. No matter how long I wait for it to cool, the first bite—"

"Can I drive home?" she interrupted and lowered her slice.

"No way!" Bobby cried.

They both laughed. She gazed at him coyly and grabbed his hand on the table. "Don't I make your life exciting?"

"Yeah. Too exciting!" he replied, rolling his eyes.

"More than Bree, right?" she demanded, her eyes locked on his. "More than Bree?"

"Your sister is—quieter," Bobby replied uneasily.

"You don't know anything about her," Samantha snapped, startling him. She raised the pizza to her mouth and bit off a large section.

They talked about school for a while. Bobby talked about his monkeys, Wayne and Garth. She said she wanted to show him *her* science project. "How about after chorus practice on Monday?"

He shook his head. "I've got band practice. We're playing in front of the whole school next week."

He told her he was thinking of dumping Arnie and Paul and finding new band members. "They just can't keep up with me," he explained.

"But Arnie is your best friend," Samantha protested.

"That's show biz!" Bobby replied.

They both laughed.

Samantha is totally crazy, but she has a great sense of humor, Bobby decided. Bree is so serious all the time, he realized.

How can twins be so totally different?

They left the restaurant without finishing their pizza. Samantha could never sit still for more than a few minutes.

Bobby asked if she wanted to see a movie. But she chose to cruise the mall. She took his hand. "I like walking with you," she whispered in his ear. "I just like being with you."

Her soft breath made the back of Bobby's neck tingle. He put his arm around her shoulders, and they began to walk slowly, window-shopping.

Samantha stopped at the entrance to a department store. "Let's go in for just a moment," she said, tugging his hand.

When she started eyeing the earrings in the jewelry department, Bobby felt his stomach tighten. "I don't like your smile right now," he told her.

Her green eyes flashed. Her smile grew wider.

"You're not going to shoplift again—are you?" Bobby demanded warily.

Samantha shook her head. "No, I'm not," she said. *"You* are!"

"Whoa! No way!" Bobby threw up his hands like a shield and started to back away.

"Come back here," Samantha ordered. "You dared

me to drive here without stopping, right? So now it's your turn. Come *here,* Bobby!"

"I'm not doing it, Sam. No way," Bobby insisted. But he stepped up to the glass display case.

"See that silver charm bracelet?" She pointed to it, tapping her pink fingernail on the glass. "I need it."

"No way. Unh-unh." Bobby shook his head. He grabbed her hand. "Let's go."

She pulled her hand free. Her smile faded. "We'll go—as soon as you get the charm bracelet for me. I'm *daring* you, Bobby. You can't wimp out on me."

He stared into her eyes, trying to see if she was serious or playing with him.

She was serious.

"Just take it from the case, and let's go," she urged, leaning close to him. Again her breath tickled his neck, exciting him. "You saw how easy it is. Now it's your turn."

He hesitated, lowering his eyes to the glass case.

"You're not a wimp, are you?" Samantha demanded softly. "You're not a chicken-livered wimp, are you?"

"No one *ever* calls me a wimp," Bobby replied seriously, his eyes on the silvery charm bracelet.

"Wimp!" Samantha teased. "Wimp wimp wimp!"

"Shut up," Bobby said sharply.

"Wimp wimp."

"Shut up. I'll get you your stupid bracelet," he told her.

He glanced toward the back of the jewelry department. There were two salesclerks, both helping customers.

He turned to check out the store exit. No security guard in sight.

He swallowed hard, took a deep breath. "Here goes," he whispered.

He grabbed the lid of the glass case with both hands, lifted it—and set off a loud alarm.

chapter

14

Caught

"Ohh!" Bobby let out a startled cry as the loud bell rang out over the store.

"Grab it! Grab it!" he heard Samantha shout.

He grabbed the charm bracelet with a trembling hand. Dropped it. Grabbed it again.

He pulled his arm back, letting the glass lid slam shut.

The alarm bell rose over the sounds of the store.

Before Bobby realized it, he was running. Running through the bright blur of colors and lights. Running through the deafening *clang*.

His heart thudding in his chest, he held the bracelet in front of him—and ran.

Where was Samantha?

He didn't see her.

He saw only the open doorway. A woman bending over a kid in a stroller. A teenage couple behind her.

"Hey—stop! Somebody stop him!"

He was out of the store now, running through the crowded walkway.

Samantha?

He turned and made his way toward the food court.

"Watch out!"

He stopped short to avoid colliding with two little girls walking with their arms around each other's waists.

He spun around. Anyone chasing him? Any sign of Samantha?

"Oh. There!" he uttered breathlessly. "Whew!"

Samantha stood right behind him, not even out of breath. She reached out and motioned for him to hand over the bracelet.

Still gasping for breath, Bobby dropped it into her hand.

"Bobby, what a beautiful gift!" she cried with mock surprise. She gazed at the bracelet, then threw her arms around his neck and kissed him enthusiastically on the cheek. "I love it! You're so thoughtful!"

She slid it over her hand, onto her wrist, and jangled it in his face. "You have such good taste, Bobby. It must have been really expensive!" She burst out laughing.

"You really crack yourself up, don't you!" Bobby said, shaking his head.

"Yeah, I do," she admitted, grinning as she examined the shiny charms.

"You're going to get us killed or arrested or both," Bobby muttered, still struggling for his heart to stop racing.

"Just trying to have some fun," Samantha replied. She jangled the bracelet. "I really love it."

"We'd better get going," Bobby urged. "They're going to be looking for us."

"Can we get a milk shake first?" Samantha asked. "I have such a craving for a milk shake."

"No way," Bobby replied, nervously glancing over her shoulder. "The security guards—"

He stopped in midsentence and let out a choked cry.

Samantha turned to follow his gaze.

"Oh, wow," Bobby whispered. "It's Bree!"

Bree stood at a store window, a few feet in front of them, staring at them in wide-eyed shock.

"We're caught," Samantha murmured.

chapter

15

Slashed

*B*ree stared at Bobby coldly. She wore a white T-shirt over faded denim cutoffs. Her hands were balled into tight fists, held awkwardly at her sides.

His mind racing, Bobby frantically struggled to think up an explanation. He glanced quickly at Samantha.

To his surprise, Samantha's expression was fearful. Her mouth had dropped open and she appeared to be trembling.

Why does she look so terrified? raced through Bobby's mind. Why does Samantha look so terrified of her own sister?

Bobby realized he was going to have to be the one to get them out of this embarrassing spot. Samantha was too frightened to be helpful.

He took a deep breath and forced a smile. "Bree—hi!" he called, waving and stepping over to her.

She nodded but didn't say anything. Her eyes were fixed coldly on his.

"Samantha and I—we were just talking about you," Bobby said cheerfully, ignoring her hard expression.

"You were?" Bree asked in a dull, lifeless voice.

"Well, it was so funny," Bobby said, thinking fast. "I mean, Samantha and I—we bumped into each other. Just a minute ago. And I thought it was you! Do you believe it? I started talking with her, and I called her *Bree*. I thought it was you."

Bree's eyes traveled to her sister. "I didn't know you were coming here tonight, Sam," Bree said suspiciously.

"I—I was shopping," Samantha stammered. "I didn't have a date or anything. So—you know me. When in doubt, shop." She let out an awkward laugh.

Why isn't Samantha better at lying? Bobby wondered. Why is she trembling? She can't be *that* frightened of Bree—can she?

"I—I was just explaining to Bobby that I wasn't you, that I'm me," Samantha continued, stammering awkwardly.

Bree appeared to relax a little. She unballed her fists and lowered her hands. Her hair was tied tightly behind her head with a blue band. She wore no eye makeup or lipstick.

She looks really outstanding, Bobby thought.

They both do. Maybe I could talk them *both* into hanging out with me tonight. A two-for-one deal. Give them both a break.

I could handle it, he thought, chuckling to himself.

"I didn't know you were coming here tonight,"

Samantha told her sister. "We could have come together."

"I was bored," Bree replied. "So I thought I'd get some new jeans. I ruined that pair, sliding in the grass at the family picnic last week, remember?"

Samantha nodded. "Well, come on. I'll help you." She took Bree's arm and started to lead her away.

"Hey, uh—" Bobby didn't know what to say. "I could come along and—"

"Bye, Bobby," Samantha called back to him. "Great running into you."

"Call me, okay?" Bree asked.

"I don't *believe* this," Bobby muttered, watching the sisters hurry away.

I came up with a perfect explanation. I got Samantha and me out of that jam.

And then they both run away like I've got a *disease* or something!

What was *that* about? Why was Samantha so eager to take Bree away?

He scratched his head, trying to puzzle it out.

Samantha is totally nuts, Bobby decided. They're *both* totally nuts.

He started walking toward the parking lot. I should drop them both, he told himself. There are so many girls at Shadyside High who are being deprived because of them. So many girls just *dying* to go out with Bobby the Man.

But there was something special about Samantha and Bree. It wasn't just their good looks, Bobby realized. It wasn't just the way they held him, the way they both kissed him so needily. It wasn't the fact that they both seemed to like him so much.

Lots of girls are nuts about me, he told himself.

It's the fact that there are two of them—and I've got them both!

The whole school is talking about me! Bobby told himself with pleasure. The whole school knows that both Wade twins are mine.

I'm famous!

At Shadyside High they'll be talking about Bobby the Man for years to come! They might even have to put a special trophy in the case in the front hallway of the school. BOBBY THE MAN, it'll say. BOTH WADE TWINS AT ONCE!

Bobby's thoughts cheered him up.

He strolled around for a bit, searching for kids he knew. When he didn't find anyone, he stopped and had a big chocolate milk shake.

Samantha has got some kind of mind control, he joked to himself as he slurped the last drop of chocolate syrup from the metal milk shake can. I'd never sit here by myself having a milk shake if she hadn't put the idea in my head.

He paid the waitress, wiped the chocolate mustache off his upper lip with a napkin, and headed to the outside parking lot. To his surprise, the lot was dotted with dark puddles. Bobby realized it must have rained while he was inside the mall.

He raised his eyes, searching for the moon. But it was hidden behind a covering of clouds.

His sneakers splashed through small rain puddles as he made his way to his car. When the red Bonneville came into view, Bobby saw at once that something was wrong.

It was resting at a tilt. A slight angle.

The car seemed lower than the other cars.

Bobby waited for a station wagon to roll past, its headlights forcing him to shield his eyes. Then, blinking away the glare, he hurried to his car.

"Whoa!" he cried out when he realized why the car looked strange. "My tires!"

The front tires were both flat.

How could he get two flats at once?

Bobby bent down, squinting in the dim light, to examine them.

Slashed.

Both tires had been slashed.

Long tears had been cut into them. Jagged tears.

Bobby ran his hand over the torn strips of rubber. A car edged past, sending up a low wave of water from a puddle. Bobby cried out as the spray of water hit his back.

He climbed to his feet, hurried to examine the back tires.

Also slashed. Also flat.

"Who?" Bobby uttered the question in a choked whisper. "Who did this?"

He leaned on the trunk, ignoring the puddles, his eyes searching the large parking lot.

"Who did this?" he shouted.

There was no one in sight. But still he felt like shouting.

How am I supposed to get home? he asked himself.

Who would *do* this to me?

He walked forward to study the front tires again, as if maybe he was hallucinating. Maybe this time they'd be okay.

No.

The tires had been cut to pieces.

Bobby angrily slapped both hands against the hood.

It took him a long while to realize that a car had stopped in front of his. He heard a car engine running, saw the long rectangle of light from headlights on the wet asphalt, and waited for the car to drive past.

But when it didn't move, he spun around and stared into the driver's window.

He recognized her at once. Saw the strange, amused smile on her face.

And guessed that she had been the one who cut his tires.

chapter

16

A Shock

"**M**elanie!" Bobby cried.

She smiled back at him, that strange, amused smile, her face half hidden in shadow.

"Melanie—you—!" he cried.

She rolled down her window. Loud music floated out from inside her car. "Bobby, hi! I *thought* that was you!" she called.

She sounded too cheerful, he realized. Since when was she so friendly? She'd been angry with him since he'd started dating the Wade twins.

He hopped over a puddle to her car and rested both hands on the door, peering in at her. She clicked off the radio. The sudden silence seemed louder than the music.

"I'm on my way to Arnie's," she volunteered. "But I had to stop and pick up something for my mom. I thought I saw you from way back there and—"

She stopped suddenly, raising her eyes over his

shoulder. "Bobby—your car!" she cried. "What happened to your tires?"

Phony, phony, phony, Bobby thought.

Does she really think I'm going to buy that wide-eyed innocence?

"Someone cut them," he murmured, studying her with his eyes.

"Huh?" Her mouth dropped open. "You mean—?"

"Someone cut them all up," Bobby said unhappily. "Can I have a lift?"

She nodded her head. "Sure, jump in." She stared hard at his car, resting so low on its wheels. "What a lucky coincidence that I came by," she said as he lowered himself into the passenger seat.

"Yeah. What a coincidence," Bobby murmured bitterly and slammed the car door shut.

After school on Monday, Bobby dropped his backpack into his locker, then started to the music room to rehearse with the band.

Arnie had called him on Saturday with the news that he and Paul wanted to change the name of the group to Desperadoes. Bobby didn't see any point in arguing.

We're going to look like total dorks in front of the entire school on Friday, he told himself. It doesn't matter if we call ourselves Desperadoes or The Rolling Stones!

On Sunday, he had spent a lot of time thinking about Melanie and the slashed tires. At first, he was convinced that she was responsible.

She's so jealous of the twins, he told himself. She

wants me back. The poor kid is so desperate, she's out of her head.

But after a lot of thought, Bobby decided he was wrong. Melanie and Arnie seemed pretty happy together. She didn't want to go back to Bobby.

Melanie, he knew, was a good friend of Bree's and Samantha's. And Melanie had certainly been angry that Bobby was secretly dating them both.

But is Melanie upset enough about it to slash my tires? Bobby wondered. Does she really care that much?

His answer was no. No way.

Girls aren't strong enough to cut tires that deeply, Bobby told himself. Girls don't know how to handle knives. No way.

It had to be someone else, Bobby decided. But who? He hadn't a clue.

Halfway to the music room, he stopped to kid around with some guys from the basketball team. Then he saw Bree across the hall. He waved to her, and she waved back.

"Wait up!" he called.

She disappeared into the auditorium, probably hurrying to chorus practice.

He turned the corner and nearly collided with Samantha. "Hey!" he called out. "How's it going?"

"I saw you chasing after Bree," Samantha said, eyeing him coldly. "You're not really falling for her, are you?"

"Huh?" He scratched his head and flashed her his best innocent smile. "No way, Sam."

Her expression softened. She grabbed his arm. "Come with me. Hurry."

He pulled away. "I'm late for practice."

"It'll take only a minute," she told him. She tugged on his hand. "Come on. I won't bite." A sly smile crossed her face. "Or maybe I will."

She pulled him up the stairs and down the nearly empty hall to the science lab in the back. The door was shut. She grabbed the knob and pushed it open.

"Your science project?" Bobby asked. "Is that what you want to show me?"

She nodded. They stepped into the large room. The lights were off.

Bobby reached for the light switch, but she grabbed his hand. Then she pressed him against the wall and kissed him. A long, passionate kiss.

When she finally pulled her face away, they were both breathless. "I like your project," Bobby joked. "You get an A."

She giggled and squeezed his hand. Bobby could hear his two monkeys chattering excitedly. In the dim light that filtered in through the closed venetian blinds, he could see them leaping around in their cage at the back of the room.

He reached for the light switch, but Samantha pushed his hand away again. "I want to show you something," she whispered.

They heard loud footsteps out in the hall. Laughing voices of two teachers. Samantha pressed her hand over Bobby's mouth. They remained frozen in the darkness, waiting for the teachers to pass.

Samantha lowered her hand and took a step into the dark room. Her eyes glowed excitedly in the dim light.

"What do you want to show me?" Bobby asked eagerly.

A sly smile crossed her face. "Remember I told you there was a way to tell Bree and me apart?" Samantha whispered.

"Yeah. I remember," Bobby replied, trying to guess what she was about to say. He grabbed her around the waist. "Kiss me again. I bet I can tell the difference."

She pushed him away. "Shut up, Bobby. This is what I want to show you. Look." She reached up and pulled her T-shirt down off her left shoulder. "See?"

Bobby leaned in closer, struggling to see what she was showing him. A tattoo. A tiny blue butterfly tattoo on her shoulder.

"Cool," he whispered.

"Bree would never get a tattoo," Samantha whispered. "Never."

She straightened the neck of her T-shirt. Then she put both hands on his shoulders and pushed him back against the wall. "I want you to drop Bree, Bobby," she said through clenched teeth.

"Huh?" Bobby reacted with surprise.

She pressed harder, pinning him to the wall. "I'm sick of this," she said sharply. "I don't care about her feelings anymore. I want you to get rid of her."

"Well . . ." Bobby hesitated.

"I mean it," she insisted. "Tell Bree you can't see her anymore. Be nice about it. Or don't be nice about it. Just get rid of her."

"I'll try," Bobby promised.

"No. *Do* it," she said, pushing on his shoulders. "I'm telling you this for your own good. I'm not just being selfish. You don't know my sister. You don't want to get involved with her. I've warned you before."

"Okay," Bobby replied softly. He wasn't sure he wanted to drop Bree. He liked her, liked her a lot. But he didn't want to argue about it with Samantha.

Samantha leaned forward and kissed him again. A short kiss, as if sealing the bargain.

The monkeys chattered excitedly in their cage. Bobby clicked on the lights. The two long rows of fluorescents flickered on.

"Have you met Wayne and Garth?" Bobby asked, making his way over to them. They hopped up and down, pleased to see him. "Look. They think I'm going to feed them."

"They're so cute!" Samantha gushed. "I love their curly tails!"

Bobby poked his finger into the cage and scratched Garth's back. "I'd take them out and let you hold one," he said, "but I'm really hanging Paul and Arnie up. I've got to go."

"But I brought you here to show you *my* project," Samantha replied. She tugged him over to a glass aquarium case on a table against the wall. "Look. My little guys are cute too."

Bobby stared down through the glass lid over the aquarium. At first he saw only the yellow sand that covered the bottom. Then he saw large red insects crawling over the sand. "Ants?"

Samantha nodded, her eyes trained on the cage.

"I don't think I've ever seen red ants before," Bobby told her. "They're enormous!"

"They're cannibal ants," she said. "From New Zealand."

"Wow. Interesting," Bobby replied, bending down to get a closer look. "What's that they're eating?"

"A dead mouse," Samantha replied.

"Yum!" Bobby grinned at her, then returned his glance to the cage. "They're doing a pretty good job. They've chewed that mouse down to the bone."

"They eat twenty times their weight every day," Samantha said matter-of-factly.

Something about the way she said it, something about the cold detachment in her eyes, the tight, almost angry expression on her face, gave Bobby a chill.

He stood up. "Hey, they're making me hungry!" he joked.

She didn't laugh.

"Later," Bobby said, heading to the door. "I've got to get downstairs. I'll call you."

"Yeah. Later," Samantha replied absently.

He glanced back to see her still leaning over the glass case, staring intently at the swarming red ants.

"Are you nervous?" Arnie asked, scratching the blond fuzz above his lip.

Bobby shook his head. "No way, man. We're as good as we're ever going to be!"

Paul laughed. "Is that a compliment or a put-down?"

Bobby laughed but didn't reply. They were standing backstage in the auditorium, waiting for their turn in the spring show.

"I just wish they'd let us tune up before we go onstage," Bobby grumbled.

"You don't have to tune up a keyboard," Paul said.

"You know what I mean," Bobby replied sharply. "What if the balance isn't right? What if my amp is too loud or too soft? What if one of the amps is busted or something? They should have given us a few minutes to check out the system."

"Yeah, you're nervous," Arnie muttered. He tapped his drumsticks against the tile wall, tapping out a rapid rhythm.

"We're on next," Paul informed them. "Right after the gymnastics demonstration."

"Are they going to pull the floor mats away so I have room to move?" Bobby demanded.

Paul groaned. "You're not going to dance around again, are you? I thought we agreed—"

"Whose band is this?" Bobby interrupted angrily. "No one named you leader, Paul."

"We don't have a leader, remember?" Arnie chimed in, stepping between Bobby and Paul. "We decided."

"We also decided we didn't want Bobby prancing around like a rooster," Paul shot back.

"Is my hair okay?" Bobby asked Arnie, ignoring Paul. "How does this look?" He turned up the collar of the bright red shirt he was wearing.

"Lookin' good," Arnie replied, giving Bobby a thumbs-up.

Bobby saw Kimmy Bass just then, leaning against the open stage door, glaring unpleasantly at him. "What's *her* problem?" he asked in a low voice. He glared back at her. "What's *she* staring at?"

"I don't think she likes you," Paul commented, grinning. "Kimmy's been bad-mouthing you all around school."

"Who—me?" Bobby stared at her across the dark backstage area. She didn't move away from the shadowy doorway.

"Kimmy's been telling everyone that you're a sexist pig," Paul said.

Bobby laughed. "She's just jealous." He shook his head. "Sorry, Kimmy," he said in a low voice. "I wish I could give you a break. But I just don't have time for all the bow-wows in this school!"

Arnie laughed and slapped Bobby on the back. Paul started to say something. But he stopped when loud applause and cheers rose up from the auditorium.

The gymnastics display had ended. Kids were pulling away the floor mats. Mrs. McCuller, the show director, was shouting for everyone to get quiet so the band could come on.

"Here we go, guys," Bobby said, adjusting his shirt collar as he headed onto the stage.

"Here come the Desperadoes!" Arnie exclaimed.

They were greeted by a mix of cheers and hoots as they stepped onto the brightly lit stage. Bobby turned to gaze out at the audience. But the auditorium was too dark to make out any faces beyond the first two rows.

Their instruments had been placed at the back of the stage. Bobby picked up his white Fender Strat and slipped the strap over his shoulder. He saw that Arnie had a nervous frown on his face as he climbed behind his drums.

Paul rolled his keyboard centerstage. Bobby bent to turn on his amp. It let out a low buzz. He turned it up nearly as high as it would go. It might drown out Paul a little, he thought, but so what?

He stepped in front of Paul. "Hey, move aside, man. You're blocking me!" Paul protested.

Bobby pretended not to hear him. He turned back to Arnie. "Ready?"

Arnie raised the drumsticks in one hand. "Let's do it."

Bobby pulled a pick out of his pocket. He strummed the pick over the strings.

A hard jolt—like a punch in the stomach—sent him sprawling backward.

Stunned, he heard a loud crackle.

The crackle became a roar.

His arms flailed helplessly above his head as his body jolted again. Again.

I can't breathe! he thought just before he dropped into a shimmering pool of deep, endlessly deep blackness.

chapter

17

Death

Bobby blinked his eyes. Gray faces floated in the misty light above him.

Gray faces, open-mouthed, eyes wide with worry.

He blinked again. The faces didn't go away.

This is death, he thought. Floating gray faces. I'm dead.

"He opened his eyes," someone said.

"He's breathing okay." Another voice.

The mist swirled above him. The faces shifted and moved.

"Don't try to sit up," someone said.

"No. Make him sit up," another voice argued.

Bobby began to recognize faces. Mrs. McCuller, her features strained. Arnie, a strange, frightened smile on his lips. Melanie, staring down at him blankly. Kimmy, her face just as expressionless as Melanie's.

"Am I dead?" Bobby's voice came out a choked whisper.

Someone laughed.

"You'll be okay," Mrs. McCuller whispered. "You had a bad shock. We've sent for an ambulance. Do you think you can sit up?"

"But am I dead?" Bobby repeated. The faces floated in and out of the mist. He had to get an answer to that question. He *had* to!

"You're going to be fine," Mrs. McCuller assured him.

"Hey—check *this* out!" Bobby heard Paul's voice from somewhere in the distance.

The faces turned in the direction of the voice.

"The amp lead wire—it's been cut!" Bobby heard Paul exclaim.

Bobby sat straight up. Paul's words brought him back to life. The mist vanished. The faces floated back.

"What did you say?" Bobby asked, squinting across the dimly lit auditorium stage.

He saw Paul near the back, holding the amp wire in one hand, examining it closely. "The lead wire is totally frayed," Paul announced. "Looks like somebody cut it."

"No *wonder* you got shocked, man!" Arnie cried excitedly.

Why is he grinning like that? Bobby asked himself. Is he just stressed out because I got zapped?

Melanie and Kimmy stared down at him, their eyes narrowed, their lips in tight lines.

Bobby suddenly pictured the slashed tires in the

mall parking lot. He stared across the stage at the frayed cord still in Paul's hand.

What's going on here? he asked himself, staring from face to face.

Is someone trying to *kill* me?

"Do you think it could have been Bree?"

Bobby pulled off his sneakers, cradling the cordless phone between his chin and shoulder. He listened to Samantha's gasp of surprise at the other end of the line. Kicking his sneakers across the room, he settled onto his bed, gazing up at the ceiling as he talked into the phone.

"Someone messed up the wire," he told Samantha. "Someone really wanted to zap me."

"Don't you think it could've been an accident?" Samantha suggested.

"The cord was cut," Bobby told her, lowering his voice as his mother walked past his room. "It was a brand-new cord. It couldn't fray overnight like that."

"Wow," he heard Samantha murmur.

"So do you think it could have been Bree?" he asked her again. "I mean, do you think she could have found out about you and me?"

"I—I don't think so," Samantha stammered. "I mean, I think she suspects something. But I really don't think . . ." Her voice trailed off.

"Well, if she did find out I was seeing you," Bobby demanded, staring up at the ceiling, "she wouldn't do anything really—*berserk*, would she?"

"I warned you about my sister," Samantha replied softly. "She—she really could do *anything!*"

Bobby started to reply, but a sound at his door made him stop and turn around.

"Bree!"

She was standing just inside his room, eyeing him intently.

Bobby's breath caught in his throat.

How much had she heard?

chapter

18

Not Samantha!

*B*ree took a few steps into the room, her eyes locked on his.

"Talk to you later," Bobby said into the phone. He turned it off and dropped it beside him on the bed. Then he swung his feet around and sat up. "Bree—hi! How'd you get in?"

"Your mom let me in," she replied. "Who were you talking to, Bobby?"

"Just Arnie," he lied. He studied her face, trying to read her expression, trying to figure out how much of his conversation she had overheard.

"Are you okay?" she asked.

He nodded. "Yeah. I'm okay. Still a little shook up, I guess."

"Oh, I was so worried!" Bree cried with sudden passion. She dropped down beside him on the edge of the bed and grabbed his hands. "I was so worried, Bobby. So worried. When I saw you collapse on the stage—I thought—I thought . . ."

"I'm okay. Really," Bobby insisted.

Was Bree being sincere? Or was she putting on an act?

She threw her arms around his neck and started to kiss him. "Oh, Bobby," she whispered. "You mean so much to me. So much to me . . ."

Bobby leaned over the bright yellow counter and sipped his Coke through a straw. Arnie, on the stool next to him, slapped him hard on the back, nearly making him spill the glass.

"Good guitar solo, man!" Arnie joked. "It was a little too short though."

Bobby glared at his friend. "Not funny."

"Hey—*short!*" Arnie cried. "*Short!* Get it? I made a pun and I didn't even know it!"

"You're not funny, man," Bobby insisted moodily, swinging his weight around on the round stool. "Give it up. I could have been killed, you know?"

Arnie spun around to face Bobby. "I doubt it, man. Not enough power in that amp to kill you. Come on, what happened to your sense of humor, Bobby?"

They were sitting side by side at the counter at The Corner, a popular hangout for Shadyside High students. It was a summer-hot Monday afternoon. The booths were jammed with laughing, shouting kids. Bobby and Arnie were the only ones at the counter.

"I'm through with the band," Bobby muttered, avoiding Arnie's eyes.

"Hey, no way!" Arnie cried. "You'll get a new guitar and—"

"You don't get it!" Bobby snapped, scowling at his friend. "I think someone tried to electrocute me, no matter what you say. Someone is out to get me, man. First my tires. Then my guitar. I've got to be real careful!"

Strong hands grabbed his shoulders from behind.

Bobby screamed.

He heard loud laughter. He spun around to face David Metcalf, a big ox from the Shadyside wrestling team, grinning down at him. "Hey, Bobby, I *love* your band!" David declared. "You guys know any other numbers?" He let out a high-pitched laugh and squeezed Bobby's shoulders again.

Bobby glared angrily at him. "How come it's so funny that I almost got fried? What's the funny part?"

David didn't answer the question. "What do you guys do for an encore? Blow up the school?" Laughing, and shaking his head, David hurried to catch up with his pal Cory Brooks at a booth near the back. "Glad you're okay, man!" he called back to Bobby.

"Funny guy," Bobby murmured sarcastically.

"You *can't* quit the band," Arnie insisted. "Hey— there's Melanie. Tell her to sit here, okay? I forgot to call home. Be right back."

Arnie waved to Melanie, then hurried to the phone booth at the back of the restaurant. Melanie made her way down the long counter. She let her backpack slide off her shoulder to the floor, and lowered herself on the empty stool next to Bobby. "You okay?"

"Yeah. Fine," Bobby replied curtly.

"Maybe someone is trying to tell you something," she said smugly.

He glared at her, then took a long sip of Coke. "Like what?"

"Like stop dating both Wade twins at once?"

The waitress mopped the countertop in front of Melanie. Melanie asked for fries and a Sprite.

Bobby rolled his eyes. "Like to repeat yourself much?" he asked her sarcastically.

She frowned at him, leaning forward on the yellow counter. The door opened behind them, letting in a blast of warm air. "Look," she said softly, "I've known the Wade twins since elementary school."

"Thought they just moved here," Bobby interrupted. He made slurping sounds with the straw, tossed the straw on the counter, and tilted the glass to his mouth to chew the ice.

"They did," Melanie continued. "But our parents have been friends forever. Our moms went to college together."

"Why are you constantly on my case?" Bobby demanded. "What business is it of yours?"

"I remember what it was like to be hurt by you," Melanie replied, lowering her eyes. "I just don't want to see them hurt."

"They're big girls," Bobby told her. "They can handle it."

"Bobby, you don't know what you're saying," Melanie said heatedly, glancing around the crowded restaurant. "Look. Your tires have been cut, your guitar was tampered with—"

Bobby grabbed her wrist. "What do *you* know about that, Melanie?" he demanded. "What did *you* have to do with it?"

"Huh? Me?" She jerked her arm free. "Me? I don't know anything about it. I'm just trying to be a friend."

"A friend?" Bobby's expression softened. "Oh. I get

96

it. You want me back. Is that it, babes?" He shook his head, laughing to himself. "Is that what all these warnings are about? You want Bobby the Man back, huh? I should've guessed!"

He leaned toward her and nuzzled her neck with his nose. "Maybe you and I should go talk about this, Mel. Somewhere private."

Melanie let out a groan of disgust. "You really are a pig, aren't you," she murmured, pulling away from him. "Well, Bobby, I know it's hard to believe, but I *don't* want you back. No way."

Bobby jumped to his feet and tossed a dollar onto the counter. "I wasn't serious about getting back with you. I was just trying to make you feel good. Tell Arnie I said bye."

He turned and strode out of the restaurant without looking back.

After dinner Bobby drove to Fear Street. Samantha met him a few blocks from her house. She climbed in beside him and gave him a kiss on the cheek.

"Where are we going?" she asked.

"I thought we'd just cruise around," he replied. "Your mom didn't mind you going out on a school night?"

"She wasn't home," Samantha replied, settling low in the seat, resting her knees on the dashboard over the glove compartment. She was wearing a silky blue tank top over white tennis shorts. "Bree wasn't home either. I think she and Mom went somewhere."

Bobby guided the car off Fear Street and onto Old Mill Road. "I didn't have much homework," he explained, his eyes on the road. "And I didn't feel like sitting home. I've been kind of restless lately. Stressed out."

"Poor baby," Samantha murmured.

"I figured you were probably bored too," Bobby said.

"You figured right," she replied, smiling at him.

Bobby turned up the air conditioner. Even though the sun had gone down, the air was still hot and damp. There was no breeze at all. The trees they passed were still as death.

"You're very quiet tonight," he told her as the trees ended and flat fields, one after the other, rolled past the windows.

Samantha sighed. "Just thinking."

"Thinking about *me,* I hope," Bobby teased. Then he added, "I've been thinking too, Samantha. About your sister."

Samantha's eyes grew wider. She turned to him. "About Bree? What about her?"

"Did she say anything to you about my guitar? About what happened at the spring show?"

Samantha bit her lower lip thoughtfully. "No. Not a word, Bobby. But she never talks about you to me. Bree and I haven't been talking as much as we used to. I—I guess you know why." Samantha turned her face to the window.

"Well, do you think Bree might be the one who—"

Samantha placed her hand over Bobby's to stop him. "Let's not talk about Bree tonight, okay? I really don't want to talk about her."

Bobby glanced at her. "Okay. No problem," he said.

Samantha is acting very strange tonight, he thought. It's not like her to be so quiet, so moody.

"I just want to ride and ride and ride!" Samantha declared, shutting her eyes and resting her head against the seat. She scratched her arm.

And as she scratched, the slender strap of the tank top dropped, revealing her left shoulder.

Bobby turned his eyes from the windshield, glanced at her shoulder—and gasped.

No butterfly tattoo.

No tattoo!

Her shoulder was smooth and unmarked.

She quickly pulled the strap back into place.

But too late.

Too late.

Bobby had already seen the smooth, bare shoulder.

He realized to his horror, *This is not Samantha!*

chapter

19

Something Smells Bad

Bobby's heart pounded. He struggled to concentrate on his driving and keep the car in the lane.

He watched her reach out to turn on the radio. It came on with a loud blast. She laughed and turned down the volume.

"Where's your tattoo?" Bobby asked.

"What?" His question, he realized, had been drowned out by the loud music.

"What station is this? Q-One hundred?" she demanded. He could barely hear her over the music, a reggae-rap song. "Have you seen the video for this song? It's so *weird!*"

"Your tattoo," he repeated. "Samantha, you—"

"What?" She couldn't hear him.

Was it Bree or Samantha? Bree or Samantha?

Samantha had the butterfly tattoo. So this girl had to be Bree.

Bree had taken Samantha's place. Bree was pretending to be Samantha.

That meant that Bree *knew*. Bree knew about Bobby and Samantha.

A dozen questions jammed Bobby's head at once: Did Samantha know that Bree knew? Did Samantha know that Bree was taking her place tonight? What did Bree plan to do? Why was Bree doing this?

He accidentally swerved the car onto the soft shoulder and bumped along the tall grass. Trying to shake all the questions from his head, he guided the car back onto the road.

I've got to find out some answers, he decided. He slowed the car, pulled it onto the grassy shoulder, and stopped. Then he clicked off the radio.

She smiled at him, a devilish smile. "Bobby, parking so early? What *do* you have in mind?"

She started to lean toward him, shutting her eyes and raising her face to kiss him.

"You're Bree, aren't you," he said.

Her eyes opened wide. She pulled her head back. "Huh?"

"You're Bree, aren't you?" Bobby repeated, staring intently at her.

She laughed. "Bobby, are you still in shock or something? Can't you tell us apart after all this time?"

"Yeah, I can," Bobby told her. "And I know that—"

"Are you totally losing it?" she demanded shrilly. "I *told* you Bree wasn't home. You know Bree doesn't know about us." She let out an angry sigh. "I don't *believe* you, Bobby. I am really hurt. How can you think I'm my sister? I mean, is that all I mean to you—just one of the Wade twins? It doesn't matter which one?"

She had tears in her eyes. He could see she was about to explode.

"But what about the tattoo?" he blurted out.

Her face twisted in surprise. "Tattoo? What tattoo? Bobby—I'm really worried about you. That shock—I think it did something to your brain."

"The tattoo on your shoulder," Bobby insisted.

"You want me to get a tattoo on my shoulder?" Samantha asked, bewildered. She touched her shoulder. "My parents would *kill* me! Why do you want me to get a tattoo?"

Bobby stared at her, confused thoughts spinning through his head. "But, Samantha—"

"Are you sure I'm not Bree?" she snapped angrily.

Oh, wow, Bobby thought. I'm in major trouble now. She's getting really steamed. How do I get out of this?

"Sorry," he muttered. "Maybe my brain *was* fried, Samantha. Let's forget the whole thing, okay?" He reached for her, but she leaned back against the passenger window.

"Just take me home, okay?" she asked, tears in her eyes. "I'm really hurt, Bobby. Really hurt. Just take me home. Now."

The next morning he saw Bree and Samantha outside their homeroom. They were standing close together, talking heatedly, both talking at once, both gesturing with their hands.

They stopped the instant they saw him.

"Hey, how's it going?" he called, waving to them. "Looking good!"

They murmured replies.

Were they talking about me? he wondered. Is that why they stopped the moment I appeared?

Were they discussing who's going to go out with me next time? he asked himself bitterly. He had spent hours the night before, lying in bed, trying to puzzle out the mystery of the tattoo. Finally he had fallen into a fitful sleep. Nothing resolved.

He made his way past them and headed to his locker to pick up some books. It was nearly time for the first bell. The halls echoed with slamming locker doors, laughter, and early morning conversations.

Bobby saw the sheet of white paper first. It was taped to his locker door. As he moved closer, he saw that it was a note.

THIS IS YOU INSIDE.

The words were large, printed in big block letters with a red marker.

As he gaped at the note, an unpleasant odor invaded his nostrils. Something smells here, he thought. Something smells *really* bad.

Where was it coming from? Inside his locker?

Holding his breath, Bobby turned the combination lock, pulled open the door—and gasped.

He saw the dark blood first.

The dark blood smeared on the locker walls.

Then he lowered his gaze to the locker floor and saw the monkey's head.

Cut off just below the chin, the monkey head rested in a dark puddle of blood. Its tiny black eyes stared up lifelessly at Bobby. Its mouth frozen open in a silent cry of terror and pain.

chapter 20

"We Have to Kill Her"

With a low, horrified groan, Bobby lurched backward.

He felt his stomach knot and then toss, and before he could hold back or move away, he began vomiting up his breakfast.

He heard startled shrieks, then cries of concern.

When he had finished, he stood leaning with both hands pressed against the next locker, struggling to catch his breath.

"Ow, wow. I see you had eggs for breakfast."

Bobby turned to see Arnie, shaking his head.

"Hey, no jokes, Arnie," Bobby choked out. He pointed to his open locker. "Don't look in there," he warned. "You'll lose your breakfast too."

"Huh?" Of course Arnie couldn't resist. He stepped in front of Bobby's locker. "What a mess."

When he saw the monkey head, Arnie uttered a startled cry. His pale face went even paler.

Then he reached down and pulled the monkey head off the locker floor. He held it in the palm of his hand and raised it to Bobby.

"Put it down, man!" Bobby screamed. "Are you *crazy?*"

"But it isn't real, Bobby!" Arnie cried. "Look—it's plastic!"

"Huh?" Bobby gaped at the monkey's twisted mouth, its black, shiny eyes. "It's not one of mine?"

"No, man," Arnie replied, holding it closer to Bobby. "It's plastic. It's just a toy."

Bobby stared at the plastic monkey head in Arnie's hand, feeling a surge of anger rise up from his chest and spread over his entire body.

Without warning, he swung his fist hard against the monkey head, sending it flying down the hall. Two girls leapt out of the way, shrieking in surprise, as the head bounced over the floor.

"Who is doing this to me?" Bobby cried. "Who?"

"Where are you taking us?" Bobby asked.

He stared out of the car window at the thick woods. The trees shivered in a strong breeze. Fresh spring-green leaves shimmered like bright emeralds.

"A secret place," Samantha replied, not smiling, her eyes on the road.

It was Saturday afternoon. Bobby had a date with Bree that night. But Samantha had called a little before noon and said she desperately had to talk to him.

Bobby had picked her up in his red Bonneville a few blocks from her house on Fear Street. Samantha insisted he let her drive. She promised she would take it easy, so he climbed out and let her get behind the wheel.

As soon as she pulled away from the curb, she opened all the windows and the moon roof. The warm wind blew through the car, making her black hair flutter behind her as she leaned over the steering wheel.

She looked very springlike, Bobby thought, in a white tank top and yellow-and-white-striped shorts. But her mood wasn't as bright as her appearance. She had barely said a word as she guided the car out of town and into the woods.

Bobby realized he had been quiet too, lost in his own troubled thoughts. He watched the trees whir by, feeling the warm sun on the back of his neck through the open moon roof.

Suddenly Samantha turned sharply onto a narrow dirt road. The car bumped along for several yards. Then she pulled to a stop under a canopy of overhanging trees.

"Why'd we stop?" Bobby asked, his eyes slowly adjusting to the shade. "Where are we?"

"We have to talk," Samantha replied, not answering his questions. She turned off the ignition and stared straight ahead. The breeze fluttered her hair.

"Talk? About what?"

"About the other night," she replied softly. "About how you mixed me up with Bree."

"Hey, I'm sorry about that," Bobby said quickly. "I—"

"I asked you to break up with her," Samantha interrupted. "Remember? Weeks ago."

"Yeah, I know," Bobby replied uncomfortably.

"Well, now it's too late," Samantha said, still avoiding his eyes, still staring out to the woods.

"Too late? What do you mean?" Bobby demanded.

"It's gone too far," Samantha murmured. "I don't want to share you anymore. It's too hard on me, Bobby. It's too confusing. We're both too confused. You know?"

"Well . . ." Bobby hesitated. He stared hard at Samantha, trying to guess what she was about to say. He always liked to stay at least one step ahead of the girls he was with. He didn't like feeling ten steps *behind,* as he did with Samantha and Bree.

"We have to kill Bree," Samantha said casually.

Bobby blinked. He knew he hadn't heard her correctly.

"We have to kill her," Samantha repeated. "We really have to."

Bobby laughed. "I don't get the joke, Samantha. You're about as funny as Arnie today."

She grabbed his hand, her eyes fiery in the shadowy light. "No joke. For real," she murmured. She squeezed his hand in both of hers. "Let's kill Bree, Bobby. Let's really kill her. She's such a total pain. You know she is."

Bobby gaped at her, startled by her growing enthusiasm.

"We'll kill her, Bobby," Samantha continued. "Then it'll be just you and me. It'll be great! So great!"

Bobby stared intently into her eyes. Is she serious? Is she teasing me? Is this a joke?

No.

No joke, he realized.

Samantha was serious. She meant it. She really wanted to kill her sister.

She let go of his hand and grabbed his shoulders. "Okay?" she demanded, pulling him close. She began smothering his face with rapid kisses. "Okay, Bobby? We'll kill her? Okay?"

She kissed his forehead, his cheeks, his chin. "Okay, Bobby? Can we kill her? Can we?"

"Okay," Bobby replied. "Let's kill her."

chapter

21

Bree Confesses

*S*amantha smiled as she raised her hands to push back her hair. The strap on her shirt moved, and Bobby caught a glimpse of the tiny blue butterfly tattoo on her left shoulder.

What is going on here? Bobby asked himself, gaping in shock at the tattoo. Samantha absently pulled the strap over it and settled back behind the wheel.

"I knew you'd agree," Samantha whispered, the pleased smile still on her face. She started the car.

Bobby stared at her. "The tattoo," he murmured. "You didn't have it when we drove around. You—"

She locked her eyes on his. "What are you talking about? You *know* I have a tattoo."

"Then Bree was pretending to be you!" Bobby told her. "Bree must have found out about you and me! She took your place and—"

"Bobby, you're not making any sense," Samantha said. "You're getting all mixed up. All the more reason to kill Bree."

She shifted the car and guided it onto the dirt road. "I want to show you a special place," she said softly.

She's totally crazy, he decided. Samantha is really nuts.

Why didn't I realize it before? Why didn't I figure it out?

She wants to kill her own sister, her own *twin* sister.

I have *got* to do something. I agreed to help her, I went along with her just to get her quiet. Just to make her shut up about killing Bree.

She's crazy. Totally crazy!

What should I do? He thought hard as the car bumped over the narrow dirt road, curving between trees, deeper and deeper into the woods until the sun was completely blocked out by the tunnel of trees.

I have to warn Bree, Bobby decided. That's the first thing I'll do. As soon as I get back to town, I'll warn Bree. And then Bree can tell her parents or the police or whomever she wants.

Samantha chuckled happily as the car hit a hard bump. She hummed to herself as she drove even deeper into the woods.

Her whole mood changed when I agreed to help her kill Bree, Bobby realized, feeling his stomach knot up. She really is a sicko.

He suddenly wondered if Samantha was the one who had been torturing him, cutting his tires, messing with his guitar, putting that disgusting monkey head in his locker.

She's dangerous, he decided. Dangerous and crazy.

He lurched forward as she braked the car to a sudden stop. "Here we are." She flashed him a warm smile. "Our own secret place."

They climbed out of the car. The air smelled fresh and piney. Bobby stared up ahead at a small, shingled cabin nearly hidden by the trees.

A wooden barrel stood against one cabin wall. A rusted barbecue grill lay on its side in the tall grass beside the barrel.

"Where are we?" Bobby asked, hesitantly following Samantha toward the front door.

"This is my family's cabin," she told him. "It's a wonderful little hideaway." She took his hand and pulled him toward the door. "We'll bring Bree here. No one will find her for weeks."

Bobby felt the knot in his stomach tighten. She has this all planned, he realized. That is so cold, so *cold!*

She stopped in front of the door and smiled at him. "It doesn't look like much from the outside. But it's real cozy inside. I'll show you."

A hornet buzzed around Bobby's head. He ducked and tried to swat it away.

Samantha laughed. "You're not afraid of bugs—are you?"

"Who, me? Of course not," Bobby replied.

"You'll have to force the door open," Samantha told him. "I forgot my key."

Bobby hesitated. "Force it?"

"Just lean on it real hard with your shoulder," she instructed. "The lock is real flimsy. It should pop right open." She gave him a playful push up to the door.

What am I doing here? Bobby asked himself. What am I doing here with this sicko?

"Go ahead," she urged sharply.

He took a deep breath and obediently slammed his

shoulder into the door. It bent but didn't give. It popped open on the second try.

Bobby led the way into the tiny cabin. Sunlight filtered in through the windows, making the bare wood floorboards shimmer. Bobby saw an old vinyl couch, two canvas lawn chairs, a couple of plastic TV tables leaning in a corner. A framed yellowed map filled with Indian names hung above the small stone fireplace.

"It's real rustic," Samantha said, moving close to him. "But it's perfect. There's no one around for miles. That's why my dad had it built here. We don't start coming out here until July."

Bobby sniffed the air. "It's kind of musty," he muttered.

"It's been closed up all winter. But it's cozy, isn't it?" Without waiting for a reply, she threw her arms around him and kissed him with real emotion.

"So we'll do it? You and me?" she whispered, nibbling his earlobe. "We'll bring Bree here? We'll kill her? And then we'll be together forever and ever?"

"Okay," Bobby replied again.

I've got to get back and warn Bree, he thought. He started to tell Samantha he needed to get home. But she pressed herself against him again and smothered him with kisses.

"Bree—I have to see you," Bobby said urgently. He whispered even though he was closed up in his bedroom. "Now."

"But, Bobby," she protested. "You're going to see me in a couple of hours, remember? You said we're going dancing?"

"Bree, listen to me," Bobby pleaded. "We have to talk. Right away."

Her voice registered surprise. "What's so important it can't wait a couple of hours? My family is eating dinner now, Bobby, and we have cousins visiting."

"Bree—please!"

"I'm sorry. Just hold your breath till tonight, okay? I've got to go. See you at eight."

The line went dead. Bobby turned off the cordless phone and tossed it onto the bed in frustration. "I'm trying to save your life, you idiot!" he cried out loud.

He began pacing frantically back and forth, thinking hard. How was he going to explain this to Bree? He didn't want to reveal to her that he'd been going out with Samantha. That would only cause more trouble.

But how could he just tell her that Samantha was planning to kill her? Why would Bree believe such a crazy story?

Who *would* believe it?

He paced back and forth in his room for a while. Then he threw himself onto the bed and stared at the ceiling, feverish thoughts spinning in his brain. His parents called him to dinner, but he shouted down that he wasn't hungry.

Finally it was time to drive to Fear Street and pick up Bree. She greeted him at the door, dressed for dancing in a silky green blouse and a short green skirt over black tights. "Good night, everyone!" she called into the living room.

Bobby saw Samantha in the kitchen doorway. "Have a good time, you two!" she called cheerily.

Bobby glumly led Bree to the car. "Are we still going dancing?" she asked.

Bobby locked his eyes on hers. His expression remained solemn. "Bree, I have to talk to you. I have something very serious to say."

"Bobby, this is so sudden. I'm too young to get married!" she joked. She frowned when he didn't laugh. "Wow, you *are* grim tonight!"

He backed down the driveway, headed the car down Fear Street for a few blocks, then pulled to a stop at the curb. "Listen," he said, turning to her. "I know this is going to sound crazy, but you've got to believe me."

Bree glanced out the window. "Why did you stop here? Beside the cemetery?"

"Just listen," Bobby said impatiently. He began the story he had rehearsed in his room. "I was cruising around this afternoon, and happened to see Samantha. She waved to me, so I stopped the car. She climbed in and said she had to talk to me."

Bree's eyes widened in surprise. "Samantha wanted to talk to you? About what?"

"That's what I'm going to tell you," Bobby replied breathlessly. "She made me drive up to your family's cabin in the woods. Then she told me—she told me—"

Bobby hesitated. Would Bree believe him?

"Samantha told me she wanted to take you to the cabin and—kill you."

Bree's mouth dropped open in shock.

"I—I'm not making it up," Bobby stammered. "I knew I had to warn you, Bree. Your own sister. Your own twin sister—she wants to kill you."

Bree stared back at him, her mouth still open. Her eyes gazed back at him blindly. And then he saw them narrow in understanding. Her features tightened. She nodded her head, as if deciding something for herself.

"I have a confession to make, Bobby," Bree whispered, avoiding his eyes.

"I—I just can't believe your twin sister wants to *kill* you!" Bobby insisted.

"I have to tell you something," Bree whispered solemnly. "You see, Samantha and I—we're not twins."

chapter

22

Jennilynn Must Be Back

*B*ree leaned closer to him, her face nearly hidden in shadow. She clasped her hands tightly in her lap. Her voice trembled as she began to explain.

"There's a third sister," she revealed, watching his startled reaction. "Samantha and I aren't twins. We're triplets."

"Wow," Bobby muttered, shaking his head. "I mean, wow."

"Our third sister is named Jennilynn," Bree continued, staring out at the Fear Street cemetery. "You must have been with Jennilynn this afternoon, Bobby. Not Samantha. Samantha was home all day with me."

"Oh, man. I don't *believe* this!" Bobby murmured. He knew how serious this was, but Bobby couldn't keep a thought from popping into his head: I've *got* to tell Arnie! Wait till he hears I've been out with *triplets*—not twins!

"Jennilynn is very dangerous," Bree continued, her eyes on the crooked gravestones beyond the cemetery fence. "We never talk about her. She was sent to live with my aunt and uncle on the West Coast."

"Why?" Bobby asked, sliding his hands around the steering wheel. "What did she do?"

"She was always terribly jealous of Samantha and me," Bree revealed. "Anything we had, she had to have—or destroy. Jennilynn just couldn't accept the idea that there were three of us and we had to share."

Bree sighed. "My parents got her therapy and everything. But it didn't help. Then, when we were thirteen, she went over the edge."

She stopped. Bobby saw that she was breathing hard. She chewed her lower lip. He could see this was really hard for her to talk about.

"What happened?" he asked softly.

Bree took a deep breath and continued. "Jennilynn locked Samantha and me in our room. Then she—started a fire. Downstairs."

"Oh, no!" Bobby cried sincerely.

"Luckily, my dad got home before we were harmed. But afterward my family knew that something serious had to be done about Jennilynn. She was sent to a hospital for over a year. When she got out, her doctors felt it would be safer for us if she didn't live with us."

"So they sent her out west?" Bobby asked, running his hand up and down Bree's trembling arm.

She nodded. "Jennilynn has been with my father's sister and her husband ever since." She raised her eyes to Bobby. "Please don't tell anyone," she pleaded. "We've moved twice since then. One of the reasons we moved to Shadyside was so the family could have a new start."

"I won't. Promise," Bobby said softly, still rubbing her arm.

"I can't believe my aunt and uncle haven't called," Bree said. "They probably don't realize that Jennilynn has come back here. I'm going to tell my parents right away. I don't know what they'll want to do about it. But I'm also worried about you. She's so dangerous."

"I'll be careful," Bobby told her.

"If you see her again, call the police," Bree urged. "Really, Bobby. Call the police right away."

Bobby remained silent for a long while, thinking hard. "Do you think it could have been Jennilynn who has been doing all those gross things to me?" he asked.

Bree nodded grimly. "Yes. It probably was her."

"But why?" Bobby demanded. "She doesn't even know me."

"She wants to destroy whatever Samantha or I have," Bree answered with a shudder. "She'll do *anything* to ruin our lives."

Bobby felt a tremor of fear run down his back. He suddenly felt chilled despite the warmth of the night.

"I—I can't believe I was with Jennilynn this afternoon," he stammered. "I really thought it was Samantha."

Bree gazed at him thoughtfully. A low howl floated up from somewhere in the cemetery. They both heard it.

"Just a cat, I think," Bobby murmured.

"I'll show you how to tell Jennilynn from me and Samantha," Bree said quietly.

"How?" Bobby asked eagerly.

Bree pulled down the collar of her blouse. "This is how you can tell it's Jennilynn," she instructed. She pointed to a spot on her left shoulder. "Jennilynn has a tiny blue tattoo of a butterfly right here."

chapter

23

Bree Is in Bad Shape

*B*obby had promised Bree he wouldn't tell anyone about Jennilynn. But he didn't care. He had to tell Arnie.

My fingers were crossed when I promised, he told himself.

He dropped Bree off at her house. Neither of them felt like going dancing. And Bree said she was too shaken about the news of her sister's return to do anything else.

He pulled his car up her driveway. She leaned across the seat and snuggled up against him. "I'm sorry about Jennilynn," she whispered. She ran her lips over his cheek. "You like me, don't you, Bobby?" she whispered. "You really like me—don't you?"

She's getting to be a pain, Bobby decided.

She was really pretty and he liked making out with her. But she was just too—needy.

And he really didn't want to deal with all this sobby

drama. Why couldn't they keep their problems in the family?

"Yeah, I'm nuts about you," he whispered. As they kissed good night, he thought about what Arnie would say when he told him about the third sister.

He drove straight to Arnie's house. He found Arnie and Melanie standing in the driveway, about to climb into Arnie's little Chevy Geo. Bobby pulled up behind them, blocking the driveway.

"Hey—what's up?" Arnie called, grinning at him.

Melanie scowled. It was obvious she wasn't glad to see him.

"We're going to the late show at the Tenplex," Arnie volunteered. "Want to come?"

Melanie flashed Arnie a dirty look. She turned to Bobby. "What are you doing here? You run out of twins?"

Bobby laughed. "Funny you should mention that. I just came over to tell Arnie some news. But I'm glad you're here, Melanie."

She rolled her eyes. "Thanks a bunch."

"You've known the Wade twins forever, right?" Bobby asked her.

Melanie nodded. "I told you that. Since we were kids."

"But you didn't tell me there were *three* sisters," Bobby said, studying her expression.

"Whoa!" Arnie cried. "Three of them! Did you go out with the third one too, Bobby? That's *got* to be some kind of record!" He slapped Bobby a high-five.

But Bobby kept his eyes on Melanie, who still hadn't reacted to the news in any way.

"Well, Mel?" Bobby asked. "Is it true? Are they really triplets?"

"Don't call me Mel," Melanie snapped. "You know I hate that."

"Answer the question," Bobby insisted.

Melanie hesitated. "I can't say, Bobby."

Bobby's smile faded. "What's *that* supposed to mean?"

"It means I can't say," Melanie repeated coldly. "Who told you there was another sister?"

"Bree did. Just now," Bobby told her, his eyes trained on hers. "So is it true?"

"I can't say," Melanie repeated sharply. "How many times do I have to repeat it?"

"Why can't you say?" Bobby demanded.

Melanie hesitated. "Because I promised," she said softly.

"So it *is* true!" Bobby cried. "You promised Bree and Samantha you wouldn't tell anyone about Jennilynn! Right? Right?"

"Maybe," Melanie said. Then she quickly added, "I mean, maybe yes, maybe no. I made a promise, Bobby. So don't ask me anything more." She gave Arnie a shove. "Come on. We're going to be late."

Arnie grinned at Bobby. "Triplets! Wow!" He turned to Melanie. "How come it's such a big-deal secret?"

"It's a long story," Melanie told him with a sigh. She frowned at Bobby. "Bye, Bobby. It's been great."

Bobby felt too pumped to go home. He cruised around town, the radio on low, thinking about the Wades.

I'm going to dump them both, he decided. Time to move on to some fresh faces. Why should I deprive all the other girls of Bobby the Man?

But then he thought, Maybe I'll drop Bree and keep seeing Samantha. Samantha is exciting. And she *loves* to make out. It would be hard to give up those long, passionate kisses, he thought.

The blood-covered monkey head floated into his thoughts. He remembered the slashed tires, the shock on the auditorium stage.

No, the Wades are too much trouble, he decided. I never bargained for a psycho third sister! Jennilynn plays too rough. I've got to get *out* of this before Jennilynn does something else. I could get killed!

I'll dump them both tomorrow. Easy come, easy go, he told himself.

But as he pulled up his drive a little before twelve, Bobby realized he was totally confused. He didn't know *what* he wanted to do about the Wades.

"Too foxy to drop, too dangerous to keep," he muttered to himself as he let himself in the front door.

He decided maybe he'd play along for a little while.

The next afternoon, an overcast Sunday with dark storm clouds rolling across the sky, Bobby met Samantha in the parking lot of the mall.

She wore a navy blue short-sleeved pullover and baggy, faded jeans. She had a Black Sox baseball cap pulled on over her hair.

"What happened last night?" Samantha demanded immediately without any greeting. "You brought Bree home so early. And she ran up to her room very upset. Did you break up with her?"

Bobby shook his head. "Unh-unh."

Samantha frowned in disappointment. "Well then, what happened?"

"She—uh—told me about Jennilynn," Bobby replied softly.

"Huh?" Samantha's mouth dropped open. She narrowed her eyes at Bobby beneath the cap.

"She told me your other sister must be back," Bobby revealed. "You know. Jennilynn."

Samantha's face paled. The light seemed to fade from her eyes. "Oh, no," she moaned. She shook her head. "Poor Bree. Poor Bree must be in bad shape again."

Bobby swallowed hard. "Huh? What do you mean?"

Samantha grabbed Bobby's arm, as if for support, and leaned against his car. "There *is* no Jennilynn, Bobby," she whispered. "We don't *have* a third sister."

chapter

24

"You're Starting to Make Me Angry"

"*T*ake me home. Right now," Samantha demanded, her eyes burning into Bobby's. "I've got to tell Mom and Dad. We've got to deal with Bree."

"But—I don't understand," Bobby replied. "What are you saying?"

Samantha uttered an unhappy sigh. "Bree hasn't done this in years, Bobby. When she was troubled, she used to make up these stories about Jennilynn, about our having a third sister. She would make up frightening stories about Jennilynn, horrible fantasies about this imaginary evil sister."

"Fantasies? They were all fantasies?" Bobby stared at her, dumbfounded.

Samantha nodded grimly. "That's how we could tell when Bree was in trouble," she said softly. "Whenever she started talking about Jennilynn, we knew that Bree was about to go over the edge."

Bobby swallowed hard and shook his head. "Wow," he muttered. "Wow. Wow."

"Drive me home, Bobby," Samantha insisted. "I'm really worried about Bree. Why do you think she told you those lies? Do you think she found out about you and me—and it messed up her mind?"

"I can't believe the Jennilynn story isn't true," Bobby said. "The way she told it—she made it so real, I—I . . ." His voice trailed off.

"Bobby, why are you staring at me like that?" Samantha asked.

"I just had a thought," Bobby told her. He reached for the collar of her pullover shirt.

Startled, she backed away. "Hey!"

"Would you do me a favor, Samantha? Would you let me see your shoulder?" he asked.

"My shoulder?" She laughed. "What's your problem, Bobby?" Her hand went up to the neck of the navy blue shirt.

"Come on, Samantha. Let me see your left shoulder for a second."

She hesitated, then shrugged. "You're getting weird, Bobby." She pulled on her shirt collar, revealing her bare shoulder.

No tattoo.

"Where's your tattoo, Samantha?" Bobby demanded, narrowing his eyes at her.

She pulled the collar back into place. "Tattoo? Get serious. You know I don't have a tattoo."

Bobby stared at her. "What about that afternoon in the science lab? Remember? You showed me the butterfly tattoo? You said it was the way to tell you from Bree?"

Her mouth dropped open. She pressed the palm of one hand against his forehead. "Do you have a fever? Are you delirious? I never showed you any tattoo in the science lab."

"Then who *was* it?" Bobby demanded shrilly.

"Are you losing it too?" Samantha asked, her expression turning to concern. "Come on, Bobby. Get a grip. I've got to get home and deal with Bree. Don't you start imagining things too!"

Later that night Bobby sat at his desk, staring at the pale blue wall, listening to the rain patter against the bedroom window. He couldn't concentrate on his homework.

It's lucky there's no school tomorrow, he thought, staring at the blank sheet of paper in front of him. The high school was closed because of a teachers' meeting. Maybe I'll be able to think clearly tomorrow. Maybe I'll be able to write my book report then.

Or will I *ever* be able to think clearly again? he wondered.

He kept picturing Samantha in the dimly lit science lab, the devilish grin on her face as she showed him the tiny tattoo. And he kept picturing Bree's troubled expression, her hands clasped so tightly in her lap as she sat beside him in the car and told him about their third sister, Jennilynn.

One of them is messing with my mind, Bobby thought bitterly.

One of them is a total liar. But which one?

Did Bree make up Jennilynn? Is the third sister just Bree's fantasy?

Or was Samantha trying to cover up her family's dark secret?

Was Samantha lying? Or was Bree?

The rain pounded against the windowpane now. Lightning flashed.

As Bobby waited for the boom of thunder, the phone rang.

"Whoa!" he cried out, startled, his voice drowned out by the thunder's roar. He picked up the cordless phone and pushed the talk button. "Hello?"

The girl's voice on the other end was harsh and impatient. "Bobby, this is Jennilynn."

"Huh?"

"I saw you in the mall parking lot with Bree this afternoon, Bobby."

"No, wait," Bobby protested, his heart pounding. "That wasn't Bree. It was Samantha."

"I know my own sister!" the voice snapped angrily. "It was Bree."

How could it have been Bree? Bobby wondered, thinking hard. *It had to be Samantha!*

And who is this?

Is it really Jennilynn?

Did Samantha lie to me this afternoon?

Why did she tell me there was no third sister? This girl's voice is different. Harsher. Much deeper. Jennilynn certainly sounds real to me!

"When are we going to kill her, Bobby?" the voice

demanded. "You promised. You promised we'd kill her. When?"

"Whoa. Hold on a minute—" Bobby pleaded.

"It's got to be soon, Bobby," she said menacingly. "Very soon. You're starting to make me angry. You're starting to make me *very* angry!"

chapter

25

Into the Woods

He tried calling Samantha the next morning, but the line was busy—and stayed busy for hours. When he called again after lunch, the phone rang and rang and no one answered.

The rain stopped just before noon, and a bright sun burned through the clouds. Bobby's parents were at work. He had the house to himself. He hoped that the quiet would help him concentrate on his book report.

He quickly found he was too upset, too confused, to write a single sentence.

He tried mowing the backyard, thinking a little physical exercise might help him forget about the Wades, about Jennilynn and her angry threat. But the grass was still wet from the night's downpour, too wet to mow.

When one of the Wade sisters pulled up the driveway in her parents' white convertible at a little after five, Bobby was almost relieved. At *last* I can get some answers! he thought.

He ran down the driveway to greet her. She had the top down. He recognized the magenta sleeveless midriff and knew for sure it was Samantha. Bree never dressed that boldly.

"Hey—how'd you get the car? I thought you didn't have a license!" he called.

She laughed. "My parents weren't home," she explained. "So I took it."

He leaned against her side of the car. "I've been calling you, Sam. I have to talk to you. I—"

"I have to talk to you too," she interrupted. She motioned to the passenger side. "Get in. I'll take you for a ride."

Bobby crossed to the other side of the car and reluctantly climbed in. "You're not going to drive like a maniac—are you?"

She grinned at him. "Fasten your seat belt," she said.

A few minutes later they were speeding along Old Mill Road, heading out of town. A cool wind blew over them as the sun began to descend behind the trees.

"Jennilynn called me last night!" Bobby told her, shouting over the roar of the wind.

Samantha kept her eyes on the road. "You mean Bree," she shouted back. "It had to be Bree."

"She said she was Jennilynn. She said—"

"I really can't hear you," Samantha shouted, placing her right hand on his to stop him from talking. "We'll have to talk when we get to the cabin."

"The cabin?" He stared at her in surprise.

"We need a private place," she said. "To talk."

She pressed harder on the gas pedal as the houses became sparser and endless flat fields came into view. Still wet from the rain, the fields glistened under the red sun as if covered with sparkling emeralds.

The wind roared over the windshield. Bobby settled back in his seat. He glanced at Samantha. Her eyes were narrowed. He leaned forward, about to turn on the radio.

The wind was blowing the strap of her midriff. Bobby nearly fell off his seat when he spotted the tiny blue butterfly tattoo on her left shoulder.

"The tattoo!" he cried, grabbing her right shoulder. "You have the tattoo!"

She turned to glance at him, a surprised frown on her face. "Of course. What's *wrong* with you?"

"But—but—" Bobby sputtered. "You didn't have it at the mall parking lot yesterday afternoon!"

"What?" Samantha raised a hand. "I don't think I'm hearing you right. I wasn't at the mall yesterday. I didn't see you yesterday, Bobby!"

She swerved into the left lane to pass an enormous truck. It blared its horn at her as she zoomed past.

Bobby covered his ears until they were past the truck. "You've always had the tattoo?" he shouted over the wind.

She nodded. "What is your problem? I showed it to you in the science lab, remember?"

The woods came into view. Samantha turned onto the dirt road that led to the cabin.

As they began to bump over the road, dark shadows rolled over the open car. Bobby realized he was breathing hard. His temples throbbed. He felt dizzy.

Was it just the wind battering him?

"You *did* talk to me about killing Bree—didn't you?" he blurted out.

Samantha turned to him with a devilish grin. "I have it all worked out," she said, her eyes flashing. "She won't know what hit her."

chapter

26

Strike One

*B*obby shut his eyes. Is this really happening? he wondered.

The car bumped along under the thickening canopy of trees. Then it jerked to a stop. Bobby opened his eyes. He saw the cabin, hidden in shadow.

The tall, old trees blanketed the sky, making it nearly as dark as night. Lost in his confused thoughts, Bobby didn't move. He suddenly felt Samantha squeeze his arm.

He raised his eyes to her. Her black hair was wild around her face. The wind had reddened her cheeks. "Let's go inside," she said softly. "We have to talk."

He nodded. "Yeah. We really have to."

He climbed out of the car and started to make his way over the wet grass to the cabin. He took a deep breath. The air smelled fresh and sweet. He saw thousands of tiny white gnats dancing in a slender shaft of orange sunlight.

He heard the car door open, then slam shut.

Samantha must have forgotten something in the car, he thought. He watched a chipmunk scampering along a fallen tree trunk. "Samantha?" He turned to the car—in time to see her lift an empty Coke bottle.

"Samantha? Hey!"

He didn't have time to duck.

She hit him over the head with the bottle.

The sound it made was only a dull *thud*.

But the pain shot through Bobby's body as if a bomb had exploded in his head.

Everything went bright white.

Then the blackest black.

chapter

27

Honey

*T*he harsh red swirls of light faded to
pink, then white. Light filtered in, misty and gray.
Purple clouds floated in a bubbling red sky.

Bobby opened his eyes.

The pain, the throbbing pain in his head, forced
him to shut them again.

Eyes closed, he tried to stand up. Something held
him back.

He tried to raise his arms. Something held them
down.

I'm paralyzed, he realized, beginning to think
clearly.

She paralyzed me.

He forced his eyes open. He uttered a soft moan.

The gray mist lifted. The cabin room came slowly
into focus.

I'm sitting up, he realized. Again he tried to stand.
Again something restrained him.

I'm sitting in a chair. I'm tied up. I'm tied to the chair.

He struggled to kick his feet. They were tied too.

My hands and feet. Tied. Tied to this wooden chair.

"Hey!" He managed to choke out a cry.

Is that really my voice? So thin, so weak?

He lowered his head. The throbbing pain lightened a little when he lowered his head.

"Oh." He saw his bare knees. His jeans were gone. So were his socks and sneakers.

He was tied to the chair, in his T-shirt and striped boxer shorts.

A low fire crackled in the narrow fireplace. He stared across the room at it. My jeans? Yes. His jeans were burning in the fireplace.

Samantha stood beside the fireplace, her arms crossed in front of her. Her green eyes caught the glow of the small fire.

"Samantha—why?" Bobby choked out.

"I'm not Samantha," she said softly. Keeping her arms crossed, she took a couple of steps toward him. "I'm Jennilynn."

Bobby shook his head. The pain that shot through his body made him cry out. "No! You're not. There *is* no Jennilynn!" he shouted. "Stop lying to me, Samantha!"

"Is that what they told you?" she asked, her eyes flashing with anger. "Did they tell you I don't exist?" She uttered a cry of disgust. "My sweet sisters would *love* to believe I don't exist," she told him, practically spitting the words."

"Stop—please!" Bobby begged.

"I'm the bad one!" she continued heatedly, ignoring

his plea. "I'm the dangerous one, the one they sent away. They pretend I don't exist. But I'm real, Bobby. I'm real."

"Okay. You're real," Bobby said, staring up into her angry face. "I'm sorry. I didn't know. I—"

"I'm the one with the tattoo!" she cried, revealing the blue butterfly. "I was the one in the science lab—not Samantha or Bree! Do you really think those two pitiful wimps would ever have the nerve to get a tattoo? No way! Only Jennilynn, only the *bad* sister would do that!"

"Okay. I get it," Bobby replied softly. The pain in his head had started to fade. He was starting to see clearly, to think clearly. Staring across the room, he saw his jeans smoldering in the fireplace.

"Let me go now," he pleaded, staring into her cold, narrowed eyes. "Let me go, Jennilynn. I haven't done anything to you!"

She scowled and stepped back to the fireplace. "My two pretty sisters—they like you soooo much," she said, rolling her eyes. She stabbed at the smoking remains of the jeans with the iron poker. "Why should they be happy?"

"But, listen to me—" Bobby started.

"Why?" she cried. "I don't want them to be happy. So—" She raised the heavy poker and pointed it at him. "So, they have to say goodbye to you."

An evil smile crossed her face. "Goodbye," she chanted. "Goodbye, Bobby."

"Jennilynn—wait!" he pleaded. "What are you going to do?"

She set the poker down without replying. She stepped behind him.

He struggled to turn in the chair, to see what she was about to do.

But he was tied too tightly.

Suddenly he felt something wet on his hair. Wet and thick.

It ran down the sides of his head, down his cheeks. He felt it on his shoulders now.

"Jennilynn—what are you doing? What is it?" he demanded shrilly.

She came around in front of him, carrying a large metal can in both hands.

"It's honey, honey," she whispered, smiling merrily at him.

She tilted the can up and let the thick yellow honey ooze down onto his lap. She poured it down his legs.

The sweet smell invaded his nostrils. The sticky liquid rolled down his forehead. He blinked to keep it out of his eyes.

"No, please!" He twisted hard in the chair, struggled to tear free, to kick out at her. But the ropes were too tight. He couldn't move.

Humming to herself, she poured it onto his bare feet. "There. All covered," she said softly, standing up and flashing him another smile. "Aren't you the *sweetest* thing?"

Panic tightened Bobby's chest. "What—what are you going to do?" he managed to cry.

Then, on the floor in front of the doorway, he noticed the glass case of red ants.

chapter

28

"Try Screaming"

"Oh, you've seen them," Jennilynn said with mock sadness. "I'm disappointed. I wanted the cannibal ants to be a surprise."

"How—how did you—" Bobby gasped. "I mean— you're not going to—"

She set the honey can down and stood in front of him, arms at her waist, admiring her work. "My sister's science project is turning out to be more useful than she ever imagined!"

"Jennilynn—don't!" Bobby protested in a trembling voice.

She laughed as she headed over to the doorway and picked up the glass case. "But, Bobby, I brought the little guys all the way out here. And they must be hungry, don't you think?"

Bobby squirmed and strained against the ropes. The sticky honey oozed over his entire body. Every part of him itched. But he ignored the itching as he watched her carry the glass case closer, close enough to see the hundreds of red ants swarming inside.

"Ants like honey, I think," Jennilynn said cheerily.

"No, please! No!"

She lifted off the glass top and set it on the cabin floor. Then she squatted on her knees in front of Bobby.

"Please, Jennilynn! Please don't!"

Holding it with both hands, she tilted the case.

Bending his head down, Bobby gaped in horror as the red ants flooded onto his feet.

Jennilynn raised the glass case a bit and poured more ants onto his legs.

"Stop! Please!" he shrieked.

She raised the case higher still to empty it on his shoulders and hair.

"Bobby, you're completely covered!" she cried in mock surprise. "Oh, boy! Look at them go for that honey!"

A thousand pinpricks of pain made Bobby squirm in agony.

"They're biting me! Help me, Jennilynn!" Bobby begged. "Please! They're *biting* me!"

The ants swarmed over Bobby's body, stuck to him in the thick honey.

"Please—help me! It hurts so much!" Bobby cried.

"Try screaming," Jennilynn advised coldly. She set down the case. "Screaming might make you feel better."

She made her way to the door, pushed it open, then turned back to him. "Go ahead. Scream. And don't worry about disturbing the neighbors. There aren't any!"

With a gleeful laugh, she disappeared through the door.

Squirming and twisting from the thousand sharp stings of pain all over his body, Bobby had no choice but to follow her advice.

He opened his mouth and started to scream.

chapter

29

Jennilynn Returns

"**M**y neck! They're biting my neck!"

The red ants swarmed over his entire body. Down his back. Under his arms.

He watched the ants slide over the oozing honey, felt a thousand stabs of pain as they chewed.

Squirming and straining, moaning in pain, Bobby felt his chest tighten. He gasped for air. "I—I can't breathe!"

He struggled to free himself. He thrust his body to one side and cried even louder as the wooden chair toppled over.

Lying on his side in a puddle of warm honey, he thrashed and kicked. Ants crawled up his neck. He felt their tiny feet under his chin.

He spit hard, blowing them off his lips. But as he gasped for air, some of them crawled into his open mouth.

"Ohh, ohhh, ohhh." He made low, moaning sounds without even hearing himself.

As he squirmed in agony, he thought he could feel each ant bite, thousands of them at once. They bit the soles of his feet, the backs of his knees, under his arms.

"Ohh, ohhhhh."

Lying on his side, he thrashed and squirmed, pulling at the ropes for hours. At least it seemed like hours. Ants crawled into his ears, onto his eyelids, up his nose.

"Ohhh, ohhhhh." Little animal moans escaped his parched throat as he struggled and tugged. But the honey made the ropes sticky, harder to budge.

Then, suddenly, one foot fell free. He didn't believe it at first. He kicked forward.

Yes!

Lying on his side, he twisted around—and slid the other foot free.

Jennilynn flunks at knot-tying, he thought. If they hadn't been coated with honey, I could have pulled free a long time ago.

Panting loudly, he struggled to his knees. His chest felt about to explode. The ants climbed around his neck. He felt their prickly legs inside his ears and on his scalp.

"Ohh, ohh, ohh."

Frantically, he slid his hands free.

"Ohhh. Yes! Yes!"

And then he began furiously trying to brush the ants away. He rubbed his face, his forehead, slapped at the backs of his knees, desperately brushed them off his arms and legs.

"I'll never stop itching! Never!"

He had to get out of there. Had to get help.

He lurched around the tiny cabin, searching for his socks and sneakers. Gone. They were gone.

"Forget them," he muttered to himself. "Got to get out. Get to the road. Get help." His heart thudding in his chest, he turned and started to the door.

"Ow!" He slipped on a puddle of thick honey and fell, landing hard on his back and one elbow.

"Got to get out. Got to get out!"

He scrambled to his feet, threw himself out the door.

Dark out now. Dark and cool.

How long had he been in there?

The soft grass stuck to his sticky feet as he ran toward the dirt road.

"Got to get help. Got to get a ride. Get home."

"Ow!" A rock cut into his foot. But he kept moving over the grass, still brushing away ants, his hands sticky and wet from the thick honey that covered his skin, his T-shirt, and boxer shorts.

He had gone only a short distance on the dirt road when he saw the twin beams of white light. Headlights.

Car headlights bouncing up the road. Coming toward him.

"Oh, no."

He knew at once that Jennilynn was returning.

chapter

30

Surprise Party

*S*hould he run? Try to hide in the woods? There wasn't time.

Bobby shielded his eyes from the bright headlights as the car screeched to a halt in front of him.

"Hey—Bobby? Is that you?"

The voice that called to him—it wasn't Jennilynn.

"Bobby? What are *you* doing here?"

Still shielding his eyes, he watched a lone figure leap out of the car and come jogging over to him. "Bobby? Are you okay?"

"Melanie!" he cried. "I—I don't believe it! How—?"

"Bobby—what happened to you?" In the light from the headlights, he saw her expression turn to horror. "What's that stuff all over you? Your pants—where are your pants?"

"Jennilynn—" he gasped weakly. "Jennilynn. She—"

"Oh, wow." Melanie shook her head, still staring in disbelief at him. "Get in the car. Quick. I'll get you to a hospital."

"No. I'm okay. No hospital," Bobby insisted breathlessly. "We've got to go to the police. Jennilynn —she's dangerous."

"Okay," Melanie agreed. "Wait. I have some beach towels in the trunk. Let me spread them on the seat. Don't sit down." She hurried to the trunk and opened it. "What *is* that all over you?"

"Honey," he told her. "I—I—" His words caught in his throat. He couldn't say any more.

A few seconds later he was leaning back against the towel Melanie had spread over the passenger seat. "How did you find me?" he asked.

Melanie stared straight ahead, guiding the car over the dirt road to the highway. "I wasn't looking for you," she explained. "I was helping Samantha and Bree. They're home alone, and their convertible was stolen this afternoon. They were pretty sure that Jennilynn had taken it. They asked me to help look for it. I remembered that Jennilynn used to like hanging out at the family cabin, so—"

"So you finally admit there *is* a Jennilynn," Bobby murmured bitterly.

"Yeah, I admit it," Melanie replied softly. "I'm sorry, Bobby. Really. I apologize. But I promised Bree and Samantha I wouldn't tell anyone about their third sister. I guess it's too late for secrets now."

Bobby was quiet, watching the dark fields roll by.

"You really are a sticky mess," she commented without smiling.

He scratched his leg. "I can't stop itching. I don't think I'll ever stop."

"We'll go straight to the police station," Melanie said. She turned to him. "Or do you think we should warn Bree and Samantha first."

Bobby thought about it. "They might be in danger," he said softly. "Jennilynn is really dangerous. Crazy and dangerous."

"Maybe we'd better warn Bree and Samantha, and *then* go to the police," Melanie suggested.

"Yeah. Okay. Good idea."

Melanie and Bobby both uttered worried cries when they saw the white convertible parked in the street in front of the Wades' house.

"The car—it's back. Do you think Jennilynn is already here?" Melanie asked, her voice trembling. She pushed open the car door. "Hurry, Bobby—we may be too late!"

They ran up the front walk. The living room drapes were pulled shut. The house was completely dark. Grass stuck to the soles of Bobby's feet. He pulled his boxer shorts up higher. They were sticky and heavy with honey.

"Bobby—I'm so frightened!" Melanie whispered. She pushed open the front door without knocking, and they burst inside.

As they made their way to the living room, Bobby heard voices. A square of light angled out into the hallway.

Bobby lurched into the living room. "Jennilynn is here!" he shouted to warn Bree and Samantha. "Look out—Jennilynn—"

Samantha and Bree jumped up in surprise. "Bobby —what on *earth!*" Samantha cried, staring at him in disbelief. "You—you're not dressed!"

Bobby heard shocked laughter. He gazed in astonishment around the room. Samantha and Bree were not alone. On the couch he saw Ronnie and Kimmy. Several other girls were seated on the floor.

They were all staring at him in amazement, staring at his honey-drenched body, at his stained T-shirt and boxer shorts, the clumps of grass stuck to his bare feet.

He opened his mouth to speak, but no sound came out.

"What on earth is going *on* here?" A man's voice broke the shocked silence. Mr. Wade strode into the living room. "Bobby—what happened to you?" he demanded.

"It's Jennilynn! She kidnapped me!" Bobby told him breathlessly. "She's here now! In your house!"

Mr. Wade made a bewildered face. "Who?"

"Your other daughter. Jennilynn. She's back!" Bobby cried.

Mr. Wade's confused expression didn't change. He stared hard into Bobby's eyes. "If this is some kind of joke or prank, I really don't get it, Bobby. Have you been drinking or something?"

"It's no joke!" Bobby cried desperately. "Jennilynn is back, Mr. Wade. You don't have to pretend she doesn't exist. I saw her. She *kidnapped* me!"

"I'm sorry. I really don't have time for this," Mr. Wade replied impatiently. "*Who* is this Jennilynn?"

"The third sister!" Bobby insisted, breathing hard.

"The girls don't have a third sister," Mr. Wade replied curtly.

Bobby heard embarrassed laughter in the room. He glanced around again and recognized more faces.

What's going on here? he asked himself. It looks like every girl I ever dated and dumped is in this room!

"Wait, Mr. Wade," Bobby pleaded. "She took me to your cabin. Jennilynn did. She dumped cannibal ants on me! She—"

"Huh? What *kind* of ants?" Mr. Wade demanded.

"Cannibal ants!" Bobby cried breathlessly.

Mr. Wade frowned. "There's no such thing as cannibal ants."

"But—but—" Bobby stammered, hearing more laughter in the room. "You can check your cabin if you don't believe me!"

Mr. Wade's eyes narrowed. His confusion was quickly turning to anger. "Bobby, we don't own any cabin. And the girls don't have a third sister! You're not making any sense."

Bobby had a sudden flash of memory. He remembered having to break into the cabin the first time he was there. Was it possible it *didn't* belong to the Wades?

"Where is this cabin?" Mr. Wade demanded suspiciously.

"I—I don't know," Bobby stammered. "In the woods. On a dirt road." He turned desperately to Melanie, who had joined Ronnie and Kimmy on the couch. "Melanie knows. Tell him where it is," Bobby pleaded.

"I'm sorry, Bobby," Melanie replied softly. "I don't know anything about a cabin."

"Huh?" Bobby gasped in shock. "You're lying! Lying!"

"Take it easy, Bobby," Mr. Wade urged. "If you've been drinking, we'd better get you home." He turned to his two daughters. "Do either of you know what Bobby is talking about?"

"No, Daddy," Bree replied quickly.

Samantha shrugged. "Beats me."

"They're lying!" Bobby screamed. "Listen to me. Maybe there isn't a Jennilynn. But one of them drove me to a cabin."

"Stop right there," Mr. Wade interrupted. "Bree and Samantha don't have drivers' licenses yet."

"One of them drove me," Bobby insisted. "The one with the tattoo. The one with the tattoo—she kidnapped me and—"

"Tattoo?" Mr. Wade's voice boomed loud in the small living room. "They'd *better* not have any tattoo!"

"Look at their shoulders," Bobby urged desperately, pointing at the two girls. "The one with the tattoo—she did it!"

"Let me see your shoulders, girls," Mr. Wade ordered sternly.

"Daddy, this is silly," Bree said. "Bobby has totally *lost* it!"

"All this crazy talk about a third sister and cannibal ants," Samantha muttered. "He needs help, Dad. He really needs help."

Both girls obediently lowered the collars of their T-shirts.

No tattoos.

The phone rang. "Bobby, you'd better get home and get cleaned up," Mr. Wade said sternly. He hurried away to answer the phone.

"You did this to me!" Bobby shrieked as soon as Mr. Wade had left. "You did it! You found out I was dating you both—and you cooked this all up! You and Melanie!"

The twins gazed at each other innocently. "We've been home all night with our friends, Bobby," Samantha said meekly. "We haven't been out for a minute."

Melanie suddenly climbed to her feet. "I warned you," she said in a low voice. "This is what you get for the way you treated Bree and Samantha, and for the way you treated all of us. You're not Bobby the Man. You're Bobby the Total Pig!"

The girls in the room—the ones Bobby had dated and dumped—burst into loud cheers and applause.

"Dating both Wade twins was the last straw," Kimmy said angrily.

"That's when we got the idea to pay you back," Ronnie added.

"I had so much fun driving you crazy, acting like a wild girl," Samantha said with a grin. "Making you think Bree and I were so, so different!"

"You got a little carried away with the shoplifting," Bree told Samantha sternly.

"Yeah. I guess," Samantha replied. "But the look on Bobby's face—"

"Hope you liked your surprise party," Melanie cut in, unable to hold back a gleeful laugh.

"This is the best party I've ever been to!" another girl exclaimed.

"Nice outfit, Bobby!" someone else remarked. Everyone laughed some more.

"You—you mean you don't *like* me?" Bobby cried in disbelief.

His question was greeted by gales of scornful laughter.

Bobby started to protest. But he realized there was no use. Defeated, he turned and slumped out of the room, their laughter ringing in his ears.

After school a few days later, Bobby started toward the music room. He was halfway there when he remembered he no longer had a band. Paul had found another group to play with. And Arnie had finally realized that he had no sense of rhythm, and had sold his drum set.

Bobby headed toward the exit, but stopped short as Bree and Samantha hurried up to him. "Here," Bree said. She slipped a small envelope into his hand.

Bobby raised the envelope and quickly read the handwritten message on the back:

"Twin sisters don't have secrets. We both knew everything from the very start. Bye."

"Bye!" Bree and Samantha called. They waved to him and disappeared around the corner.

Bobby sighed and tore open the envelope.

Inside, he found a small paper temporary tattoo. A blue butterfly.

About the Author

"Where do you get your ideas?"

That's the question that R. L. Stine is asked most often. "I don't know where my ideas come from," he says. "But I do know that I have a lot more scary stories in my mind that I can't wait to write."

So far, he has written nearly three dozen mysteries and thrillers for young people, all of them bestsellers.

Bob grew up in Columbus, Ohio. Today he lives in an apartment near Central Park in New York City with his wife, Jane, and thirteen-year-old son, Matt.

THE NIGHTMARES
NEVER END . . .
WHEN YOU VISIT

NEXT: *THE THRILL CLUB*

Five kids from Shadyside High have formed a new,
scary club . . . the Thrill Club. Every week, Talia
Blanton reads a horror story sure to send chills up
everyone's spine. Her stories are so good, they almost
seem real. And she even gives her friends starring
roles.

But then Talia's stories start to come true. Two
members die gruesome deaths. Now the Thrill Club
starts wondering about Talia. Why does she always
use real names? And who will be next?